Beautiful
Curse

Beautiful Curse

Beauty is in the eye of the beholder. Beautiful people don't agree with every reason behind what is said makes them beautiful, and some don't even accept what is said is not supposed to be beautiful when really, it is just that!

Donna Christopher

Beautiful Curse

Chosen Destiny Books

Copyright © 2018 by Donna Christopher

Dedications

I dedicate this book to all young girls searching for love, needing to feel love. I love you! God loves you! To all the girls who has ever been abused or going through abuse, don't you dare give up. You are valuable, your life is valuable, your dreams are valuable, your purpose is valuable. Find your strength to fight for survival and overcome because your best is yet to arrive. You are perfect in God's image and I pray for your gifts, talents, purpose and your uniqueness to shine bright for all the world to see.

I dedicate this book to the young men who respect and protect all females young and old in your life. Your greatness is appreciated, your strength is appreciated, your gentle kindness is appreciated, your protection is appreciated. You my dear friend in all your amazing qualities God designed for you in His image to be the best you for the women around you, you are greatly appreciated!

Your Beautiful Curse just may be the foundation to your Purpose God has planned for your life. No's don't mean never, and closed doors just mean the journey may take a little longer with a little more work. Don't ever give up on yourself, don't ever give up on your dreams! YOU MATTER

Acknowledgements

For my amazing, wonderful loving husband, Chris Burns, your love for me is amazing and I am forever grateful for all that you do to love your family, protect your family, provide for your family. You are my greatest blessing of love, you are my best friend, you are the love of my life now, tomorrow and forever. Thank you for being my Mr. Right-Now, Mr. Tomorrow, Mr. Forever, my lover and my friend, my shoulder to cry on, and most of all for supporting me and my dreams. Life with me of course is fun and entertaining but even when it was frustrating and stressful, you my love have always been there for me. Thank you a million times more! My King, thank you for all your support with my writing career. I appreciate you for keeping me on my toes and believing in my dreams. Your support means everything to me. I love you forever my King!

For my children, thank you for listening to my many story ideas that often explode from my imagination. You all are the first to hear my ideas and you listen attentively and encourage me along the way with every idea. Thank you, my darling loves. Your forever support means everything to me. I hope that I have been a great mother to you all, guiding you to your greatness, your purpose in life that God has ordained for you. I love you all whole heartedly. Even though most of you are now grown and you don't need me as much as when you were younger, I will always be here. You are blood of my blood, flesh of my flesh, and own a major piece of my heart, always and forever. You are mines and I am yours. My children, I love you! May God always protect you and guide you towards the greatness he has designed for your amazing life.

Momma, may you rest in Heaven and always watch over me. I hope that you are one of my many angels that God has protecting me, looking out for me, and watching over me. God gave me to you for a reason and I thank you for loving me as you knew how and raising me as your child with what you were equipped with as a person and as a mother. Thank you for giving me life. I hope you are smiling down happy of the young lady, the mother, and the person I have become. As a mother I now know that when we have children, we are often overcome with the fear of how we will survive parenthood and we hope that we will do better and be better than our parents, giving more to our children than what we experienced. I know you gave more and did better than you received and did the best that you knew how. I learned a lot from you and take each lesson learned as a blessing that helped mold me and change my life for the better. I love you momma! May you rest in peace.

Always remember to love yourself more, care for yourself first, and dream an amazing dream that you work hard to make your reality. If you are not your best you, you can't give 100% to anything else or anyone else. Regardless of your past, your future is still waiting for you to make moves to make it brighter and better. It's up to you to make the effort to be better, do better, and not allow your past to define who you are today or who you will be tomorrow. Pray often, plan daily, and go make your dreams come true!

Books by Donna Christopher

Love Never Fails Series:
Love Never Fails – Book 1
Naked Truth of Love – Book 2

Writing Blueprint

Beautiful Curse

A mother's love is a love that is so special and so unchanging. A mother's love for her child is unconditional. No matter what a child does, the love never changes. You can never replace a mother's love or their bond they share with their child. There is no war that is too big that she wouldn't fight to protect her child. No pain to painful that she wouldn't wish she could bear instead of her child. With every heartache a child endures a mother would replace a piece of her love to endure and go through their pain. A mother's love is real, is true, is unconditional. A mother's love should be cherished and never taken for granted. And a mother should never bring harm to their children. Instead love, protect, teach with love, be kind, be caring, discipline with love, provide with love, and act with love.

Beautiful

Curse

Chapter 1
Don't tell anyone, or else...

"What are you doing? Why are you in my bed? Why are you on top of me?" I remember asking the teenage boy in a scared whisper. "Get off me, you are heavy," I said, hoping he would move and get out of the bed where I was sleeping.

"I won't be long. You are just so pretty, and I like you," he said.

But I was only six years old. I didn't know what the hell he was doing laying on top of me. I saw him come in the room and open the top drawer of his sister's dresser. He was looking for something that wasn't his I'm sure. But I thought, maybe his sister told him to go through her belongings.

I was trying to mind my business and just watch. Next thing I know he got in my bed and laid his heavy body on top of me moving his body around and kissing the side of my face.

"I'm going to tell, get off me," I said again a little louder.

My brother heard me from the next room where he was sleeping. "Ava, are you ok?" I heard him ask, but I was afraid to answer because I wasn't ok, and my brother was just a year older than me.

"Shut up and go back to sleep. Mind your own business before I come in there," the boy yelled back at my brother.

"That's my sister. You better not do nothing to her."

I could tell my brother was mad by the way he yelled back at the teenage boy that was still laying on top of me.

My brother always had my back no matter the situation. I didn't want him to get hurt though. That boy was about thirteen or fourteen and I knew he could hurt my brother if he wanted to. They always picked on my brother and tried to get him in trouble.

We were staying in a strange place, in a temporary foster home because my mom was sick. We hated it there. They were not nice to us at all. None of the kids nor their parents. One day the foster parent's real kids made my brother use the bathroom in the basement closet. He had to use it bad and they kept telling him he couldn't go upstairs. They told him it would be ok for him to just go in the closet, that they would clean "it" up so he wouldn't get in trouble.

Boy did they lie. As they always did. But we were just six and seven years old. An age where kids typically believed most of what older people told them.

He definitely got in trouble. Their parents, our foster parents, tried to drown my brother in the bathtub. The entire time I could hear him scream, calling out for help and I couldn't help him. They kept telling me not to tell anyone. They said that he was in trouble for doing something bad and that's why they were doing what they did, to teach him a lesson. I was only six. I couldn't do anything.

The boys were the meanest.

The teenage boy left out of my bed knowing that my brother knew he was in there. "You better not tell anyone I came in here or else," he said.

Or else what?

He didn't bother me for the rest of the night. The next morning the parents and her kids were all gathered in the living room. I was playing with my brother. They asked me to come in the living room where they were. Everyone was in there except my brother and they wouldn't let him come into the room with me.

I walked in the room slowly and they closed the door behind me. "Ava, is there anything you want to tell us?" the mom asked me. I was clueless as to what she was talking about. Could it be about her son coming into my room laying on top of me, kissing me last night? I wanted to ask but I kept thinking about his words to me, "or else."

"No ma'am," I replied. I was confused and scared. Being in a room with a bunch of strangers was scary enough, but her mean son also told me not to tell anyone. He was looking at me real evil like.

"Are you stealing in this house?" she asked.

Stealing really? I was only six years old. I didn't care about anything much to steal anything. "No ma'am, I have not stolen anything," I calmly said to her.

"You are lying to us. We found shoes in your bottom drawer in your room and we found gum that doesn't belong to you under your pillow," she spoke those words to me in an intimidating hostile tone. All I could do was stand there scared not knowing what to say. It sounded like I was guilty by default, and nothing I could have said would have been considered to be the truth. My interrogation was simply a formality before the punishment.

"Yeap, she took your gum," the teenage boy said that was in my room laying on top of me from the night before. Why would he lie?

"I knew it was her. You little thief. She took my gum momma whoop her," his sister said. She sounds mad, but I didn't take her gum.

"I didn't steal anything, I don't know about any shoes. I haven't seen any shoes." I was pleading my case.

The momma, daddy, their two sons and their two daughters were in the living room and my brother couldn't save me. No one could save me. I knew I was about to be in trouble for something I didn't do. I didn't want my head pushed under the water. I didn't want them to drown me or try. I didn't want a whooping. I didn't do anything.

Momma!

"She is lying, and I saw her go in that drawer last night when I passed the room." Why is this boy lying on me? He knew he went in that drawer then laid his body on top of me. That's it. He had to have been the one to put the gum under my pillow when he was kissing me. Why else was he in the room. Is he going to tell them what he did to me? He should be the one getting in trouble. I should tell on him. But I was still scared to say it.

I was scared of what he would do to me.

I was scared they wouldn't believe me.

I was scared to get a whooping.

I was scared he would hurt my brother.

I want my brother.

I'm telling.

"That's a lie. I saw you in the drawer and maybe you put the gum under my pillow when you laid on top of me kissing me last night." They were all quiet looking at him. For a moment, I thought they would believe me and he would be in trouble.

He looked nervous and squint his eyes at me. "She just keeps on lying. Momma she needs a good ass whooping." He was trying to get out of what he did to me.

She looked at him and I thought he was about to be in big trouble, but instead she ignored the curse word he said and seem to not care about what he did to me. She turned her attention back to me, "Ava that is a lie, and don't you ever repeat that to anyone else ever again or you will get another whooping, worse next time for your filthy lies." She was pissed off at me and I was telling her the truth.

"It's not a lie. He did lay on top of me," I said in a quiet voice. Tears fell down my face because I knew no one believed me.

I knew he would get back at me for telling the truth.

I knew my brother would be punished too for me telling what he did to me.

"That is enough of your lies. I don't want to hear another word. I told you not to ever repeat that." She was really mad. Her husband just looked at her before she started to walk towards the door. "Come on we are going to show you the shoes you stole and put in the drawer."

She grabbed me by my arm and pulled me as we walked out of the living room and into the room where I slept. There was a set of bunk beds and another bed. I slept in the bottom of the bunk bed and her daughters slept in the other two beds. I saw my brother standing close to the door looking at my sad face as I walked towards the bedroom. They told him to stay where he was. We all walked into the bedroom and they closed the door. All of them were in there except for my brother. They opened the bottom drawer and it was empty with nothing but some shoes that were so big I could put my feet inside them twice, maybe three times.

"Those are not mine they are too big for me," I said. I was so sincere and just knew that they would believe me because the shoes were obviously too big. I was hoping they would realize that I didn't take those shoes and didn't put them in the empty drawer.

"You are such a liar," the daughter said.

"Pull your pants down you are getting a whooping," the mother said.

I started crying. I didn't want a whooping and didn't want to pull my pants down in front of all those people. She didn't care. She pulled them down herself and started whooping me with a belt like she was a crazy woman. I was screaming and jumping around. It hurt. She must have hit me thirty times or more. I was crying so hard I couldn't catch my breathe. Her kids were laughing. They laughed at me getting the crap beat out of me for something I didn't do. She didn't tell them to stop laughing either. She was enjoying the tears that fell from my eyes and the whips she was leaving on my body. How could foster parents be able to abuse kids? I knew this was not right, but I was just a kid. I couldn't save myself and neither could my brother.

I was suffering pain for something I didn't do. I was suffering pain for something someone else did to me. He didn't get in trouble for laying on me. I was getting a whopping for telling on him. I should have kept quiet. That's what I thought as a little kid was the only thing that could have saved me from pain.

After it was all done she told me to go in the bathroom, clean my face and get in the bed until she told me I could come out. I did as I was told. When I came out of the bathroom the door was closed, it was dark in the room. No lights were on and I was afraid to turn them on. The windows were covered, and no light was coming through, but I got in the bed as they said. A little while later my brother snuck into my room and checked on me. He told me he knew I wasn't lying and he was sorry I got a whopping. We both decided we wanted to go home but knew that wasn't going to happen until our mother came for us.

I tried to tell them what that boy did to me. It made me uncomfortable and all they said was that I was telling a lie, for me not to repeat it to anyone ever. What was I supposed to think at six years old? I never said anything more about it. Not even to my mom during our supervised visits.

I wished my mom wasn't sick, I wished she could have taken us home that day. All we could do was hope she would get better soon. We hated being in that place. They started making us sleep in the basement, sometimes it was pitch black. They would go outside and bang on the walls and scare us. Tell us that a monster lived in the closet next to our bed and under the bed. They told us not to get out of bed until they told us to or the monsters would eat us. Me and my brother tried to stay up until our eyes were too tired and we fell asleep laying up under one another holding on tight.

They always said, "don't tell anyone," and we never did as kids. Even though we hated being there, we knew if we said something about how they treated us, we would be in trouble. I guess we thought we would always be in trouble if we ever said anything to anyone, so we just didn't tell anyone.

Not our mom.

Not the case worker.

No one.

That was the worse three months of our young lives living in fear and being tortured living with strangers who were paid to care for us. We needed our parents to protect us. We needed someone to care. We needed someone to come rescue us from evil. Pure evil people. We survived with the love from one another, sister and brother, until the day our mom was able to take us home.

We never spoke about our experience to our mom or anyone for that matter besides our siblings and friends as we got older. We should have said something. We should have told someone about the horrible things they did. I mean who gets in trouble for leaving air in the bread bag when the bread is still being passed around the table? They found any reason to punish us when they were the ones who should have been punished for abusing two innocent children.

I know there was a lesson for me in all of that, but I can't see pass the abuse of a child. Parents should protect their children from strangers and the corrupt system where bad foster parents exist. They should have been monitored, they all should be monitored to keep bad people from doing horrible things to innocent children.

Don't tell anyone.

Those words stuck with me even as I got older. Don't tell anyone...

Or else...

Chapter 2

I could have Died

I was at home with my mom and I remember the day I felt so weak. I couldn't and didn't want to do anything. I didn't have an appetite to eat, a desire to play, or even get up and interact with anyone. I didn't even have the energy to talk. The things I use to do I had no desire to do.

My mom knew something was wrong when I continued to sleep and lay around not wanting to move. When she finally decided to check to see what was wrong, I was burning up when she touched me. I had a fever of a hundred and four and she couldn't get it to come down. She panicked. She took me to the emergency room hoping it was something simple that antibiotics and rest could cure. But when she heard the results she was devastated.

I was seven years old and I didn't know what none of anything they were saying to my mom meant. I remember them saying they needed to do more test to confirm what they told her. That test was one I would never forget.

I screamed at the top of my lungs crying, yelling, pleading for them to stop. Calling for my momma. I wanted her to save me. It hurt so bad. Excruciating. It took seven doctors and nurses to hold my body down to keep me still as they stuck a gigantic needle in my back to draw fluid from my spine. (I think that's what they said they did.) All I know for sure is that shit hurt like hell. I remember the pain. I wouldn't wish that pain on anyone. When they were done, blood was all over the table. My blood.

My mom was hysterically crying. I remember her face looking through the small window when they told her she couldn't come inside to be with me while they performed the procedure. She looked scared. I couldn't even mouth the words "mom I will be fine" to her as they rolled me inside the room. I was too weak. I was so weak that I don't even see how I was able to scream so loud, but I did. That pain. I remember that pain.

I don't even remember the waiting period. I was sleep as my mom waited with me to get the results that I had Bacterial Meningitis. I don't remember anything after that until I was waking up in a hospital bed in my own room. Well, I had a roommate, but her bed was on the other side of the room with a curtain in between us.

My body hurt so bad. I don't know what happened before I got in that room. I don't know if they had to do any more test or what before I got to the room. After I was awake, I remember them asking if I wanted anything and I told them paper and crayons. I started writing down what I wanted to say on paper for my mom and the doctors. I don't know why. I could talk. Guess I was still weak. Everything was a blur as to how I got to that point.

I remember talking. I remember the nurse giving me some medicine and making me turn in my bed to face her. My body hurt so bad to turn towards her. I didn't want to move. She made me. Said I had to move so I could start getting better and my body won't be so stiff. I was seven, I had to do what she wanted me to. After I took my medicine I asked her, "where is my momma?" She made me turn to the opposite side of the bed. I turned my body even though it was so painful because I needed to see my momma.

She was smiling when I turned over. She was happy I was getting better. She was happy I didn't die.

I could have died.

The doctors thought I was gonna die.

My mom was hoping I wasn't going to die.

God had plans for my life I couldn't die. He saved my life. When the odds were against me living, God saw differently.

I was seven years old and I didn't know what was going on besides me being sick. But what I do know is that someone more powerful than my momma, more powerful than the doctor's, more powerful than anything living had a purpose for me and I wasn't going to die.

My God had a purpose for me to live beyond the age of seven. That fatal disease was not intended to take my life.

Fatal disease!

The odds were against me surviving.

It happened yes, me getting that fatal disease. But it was not intended to take away the seven years I had spent living, but to give me life beyond that hospital bed. To give me life beyond that disease. God had a plan for me. It was up to me to live, learn, go through life and figure out his plan for me. Figure out his purpose for me.

But why the foster care situation?

Why the bacterial meningitis?

Why the hell did all the shit that happened to me in my life happen? The foster care and the fatal disease I survived was just the beginning of all the bad that happened to me during my lifetime, that should have counted me out in life. But it didn't, and I am still here able to tell my story.

Chapter 3
The Move from Hell

I remember like it was yesterday. It's one of those things that you just cannot forget as a kid. Especially the bad things that happened because of it. We lived in a decent area at the time. Nice neighbors and normal kids that came around us. No extra drama. We were safe, and we were happy growing up as normal kids.

That night smoke filled our home. My brother woke up to use the bathroom and saw the thick smoke all through the hallway. He woke our mom, and once she realized the house was on fire, she hurried to get us out of bed and out of the house as the fire quickly started to spread from the kitchen.

We stood in the living room with her while she tried to wake her boyfriend. Her boyfriend was drunk, passed out on the sofa in the living room. She couldn't wake him. She couldn't lift him. We stood waiting for her to go outside with us. Next thing we saw was my mom balling up her fist and punching him in the face.

As a kid we didn't understand why she punched him, but what we did understand was that the house we lived in was on fire. He got up quickly when he realized what was happening. We stood outside in pajamas watching the fire engulf our home, watching as it burned the very space where we moments before laid our heads. We had on our night clothes wrapped in blankets given to us by our neighbors watching our home burn as the firefighters started putting out the flames. All of our neighbors were awake and outside with us. We stood there motionless, not saying anything to anyone, watching the commotion.

My mom was living on section eight at the time and that meant we had to move asap. There was no staying somewhere temporarily then moving back in. We were homeless that night and we depended on our mom to protect us and take care of everything. With no money, she depended on her boyfriend. I am not sure where everyone stayed that night, it's a memory that is faint in my mind. I remember some of us ending up at my mom's boyfriend's house until she got her own place.

Weeks later when we finally did move, we were happy to have our own place again. It was in a building with other apartments that were very close together. It was a lot of families living there. We thought it would be exciting to have a lot of kids to play with that were all close by.

We didn't have much moving in. The fire burned just about everything we owned. Someone gave us some beds and some clothes to wear. My mom tried to wash the smoke out of our old clothes, but they were beyond salvageable. But we were happy in our new home. We had our mom and each other. As a kid, it didn't take much for us to be happy. Everything seemed to be going well until reality set in.

Reality of being in an unfamiliar place filled with people who didn't have a whole lot to care about. We were surrounded by drugs, gangs, killings, and rape. Then we had to go to school with kids who experienced life the hard way, seeing bad stuff happening, and experiencing it at a young age. This was different for me, for all of us. As a little girl, I didn't know what was ahead of me. My mom was no help preparing me for the journey. After all, we didn't have a choice in the matter of where we stayed. We didn't have a choice about anything at all.

Making friends was not hard for me but making true friends was scarce where we lived. I not only had to deal with being the new kid, I had to deal with being the new kid that was also the new girl that was beautiful. Light skin, curly hair and beautiful. The girls hated me, and the boys loved me. I felt like I was a beautiful curse. I didn't welcome the new attention I received from the boys and I didn't like that people didn't like me for being me.

At that point, I just wanted to be left alone and stay to myself. I didn't bother anyone, and I didn't want anyone to bother me. That was not the case. I had to fight girls who were jealous of me.

They picked fights with me for no reason at all but to prove a point to themselves and those that were bystanders. I had to fight boys who picked with me because they liked me and that was the only way they could be close to me. I had to fight when I didn't want to and had to witness fight after fight all around me, kids being mean to kids for no reason at all besides the simple fact that they wanted to. Grownups arguing and fighting like wild cats and dogs with no home training. This new place was no fun at all.

This new place was not so nice.

This new place was not welcoming.

This new place was full of crime, hate, jealousy and so much more bad that I had yet to experience.

I had to experience bad things that I wish I didn't have to experience. I had to see bad things that I can't erase from my mind, wishing I could simply un-see every bit of the torcher my eyes, my mind suffered. At times, I didn't feel safe, not even in my own home with the doors and windows locked. At times, I didn't feel loved, that place didn't seem to know what love was. At times, I felt alone. Scared and all alone.

At times, I would escape into my own imagination wishing that I was anywhere else but where I was. I lived there, in my imagination. I always came back to reality though. I didn't have a choice. Reality knocked at the door of our home. Reality was at every corner in the neighborhood. Reality was at school. Reality was everywhere around me.

A reality I didn't want to live. God has a way of taking us through things in our life that we don't understand. At that time, we never understand, but instead we wanted to fight and run far away from the pain, from the memory, from the reality we were forced to face. Memories that will always remain.

When our home was burning down I never imagined moving somewhere that would change my life. Now, living in this new place, I only wished the fire didn't happen. I wished that my brother would have awakened sooner. I wish my mom would have never been cooking them damn chitterlings. I wish they wouldn't have been drinking. Maybe she would have remembered the stove was broke and the knob had to be turned just right to really be off. Off wasn't off. Off was - you better not fall asleep or you will burn the damn house down cause your drunken-mind won't know off really is staying on.

The only good thing that came from our move was that we all made it out alive, unharmed. I was so thankful we all made it out alive but that still didn't change the fact that moving to the hood was hell for me. I was now living a completely different life-altering life. No matter how much I tried to hide in the walls of my room, listening to my music, New Edition, the quiet storm, or whatever the latest R & B that was playing on the radio, the reality of the life I was now living was real. The memories of what I experienced will always remind me of that horrific time in my life.

A fire.

Chitterlings burning on the stove.

Broken stove.

Memories of the fire taking our home.

The destruction of that fire lasted beyond the burning of the home we lived in. It carried over into our lives beyond that point. The destruction of that fire lasted beyond that night we stood outside in our pajamas watching as the home we lived in burned nearly completely to the ground, a home we would know no more. A home we would never call home again

The destruction of that fire started a chain reaction of destruction in life. A chain reaction of bad things happening, a chain reaction of a life experience opposite of what we had before.

Chapter 4

The Neighbors House

I was only twelve years old when my innocence was taken away. My beauty was a blessing and a curse, at least that is how I often felt back then. I didn't have anyone to protect me or teach me. My brother had my back always, but he was only a year older than me. Not much he could teach me and only so much he could protect me from. My sisters were younger, I was supposed to protect them. I was their protector.

My father wasn't in my life. And a lot of the men that my mom had around seem to lust after her daughters. They became enemy number one. I can only think of a couple who were good to us, but they didn't stay around long enough to matter, just long enough for me to crave the love and care from a father who would never leave. My mom was not happy with herself and that lack of happiness came off as hatred at times. Not much love you can give to someone else when you don't love yourself.

My siblings and I grew up in the hood most of our childhood life. My mom was a single parent raising five kids on her own. It was hard enough not knowing love from your own parents. She would say that her parents never said I love you and she never felt love from them. Then she turned around and had children of her own that craved love, the same love I am sure she once craved from her own parents. Seemed to be impossible for her to give love. I guess it's hard to give something you never received or was never taught to give.

I can't recall not one I love you growing up, not one hug, not one good job, not one word of encouragement and not one mother daughter moment.

Wait….

Actually I do have a memory…

I was about five years old and I remember riding the bus with my momma and we were eating

Cheetos and my fingers were all messy. I don't know where we were going but I remember her saying, "let's race and see who can get their hands clean the fastest." Being the competitive person that I am now, I know back then was no different and I was going to win. She started licking her fingers clean so I quickly took both of my hands and wiped them down the front of my white pants I wore. Need I tell you how pissed off she was. That was a mother daughter moment that went sour quickly. It's funny to me now when I think about it, but she was red hot mad at me and I was definitely in trouble.

I still loved her, she was my mother. No matter what I was going to love my mother. She just didn't know how to give love back to me in the many ways a child needed, that I needed. Especially the love that a daughter needed. I had a bed to sleep in and food to eat. Most importantly, she gave me life. I guess that was her way of loving us. She provided what we needed to survive because that's all she knew. Providing the necessities was her love.

We were a mixed race, my mom was white and daddy was black. Trying to fit in to a society that teased us because of our race was hard, and my mom couldn't relate, couldn't help us cope. We lived in a predominate black neighborhood with a white momma. I guess you can imagine the jokes, the hateful remarks that we received because we were considered to be different.

My mom had a taste of prejudice when she got pregnant by a black man and tried to take home a black baby. She said her father disowned her. Where is the love in that? He later came around several years later, but I remember one day he babysat us and for no reason took a wooden cutting board that had a handle on it and whooped us leaving huge marks on our body for no damn reason. I was little, but it was traumatic enough to remember. My mom cussed her dad out and promised us we would never be left alone with him ever again. We didn't understand what all the black and white prejudice stuff was back then, we were just kids. But you best believe I know now what that was about. My granddaddy had to learn to love his mixed grandchildren. He eventually fell in love with us and accepted that we were just as much a part of him.

Even though we didn't receive as much love as we desired, we had a lot of it to give.

When I was a kid I was teased and called names such as Zebra and Oreo. Was told I was in a category all by myself. I was alone and felt that way a lot of the times. Sometimes I even felt like my mom hated me because my twelve-year-old body was very well developed with curves that demanded attention. My body was not the body of a twelve-year-old but more like a grown full developed woman. I could feel her jealousy. My titties were perky and large, and I had a big butt and thick thighs. She hated when men tried to come on to me before coming on to her. She would get mad yelling my age to them but quickly calm down when they turned the attention towards her.

I couldn't help the way I looked. I didn't ask for the attention. I even wore old baggy raggedy clothes. We were poor and didn't have money for clothes anyway, not that it would have made a difference in how I dressed. I had no style, no one to teach me about fashion. We didn't get magazines or have a television that worked good enough to watch and observe.

I was hated by the girls who thought they were the shit until my light skin and long hair came along. They would even pull my hair say it was weave before weave was even popular. They would say, "she thinks she is fye cause she light skinned with long hair," but really, I didn't. I had no style what so ever at twelve. They picked fights with me because I was a threat to the attention they received from the boys. I had to fight a lot back then or should I say learn how to fight them back before they stopped. I never had to fight before then, besides wrestling with my brothers, but that was all play and no harm. Yes, I was a real tom boy with titties. I didn't even want any attention from boys. I hated when they would give me attention because I quickly learned in school from the other girls that if you had a boyfriend you had to have sex with them. What? Really? I didn't know what sex was about and I was surely not doing that.

My mind had a million and one thoughts when I heard them little girls talk about boyfriends and sex and discovered they were having sex with their so-called boyfriends. Twelve and thirteen-year-old girls were doing grown woman things that they shouldn't have been doing. My virgin ears were learning some very explicit information that I could have been spared. At that moment, hearing about what it meant to have a boyfriend, I decided I could do without one. I was not about to have sex just to have a boyfriend. No thank you. I knew nothing about sex, had no clue what to do or how to perform the act of sex. They even said it hurt the first time. Why would I want to allow someone to deliberately hurt me on purpose? Even though I had no love at home, sex just to have a boy love me was not in my radar of anything happening anytime soon.

That didn't stop boys from trying to get in my pants though. Once they learned that I was not a hot momma eager to have sex just because a boy lied and said they liked me or loved me, they stopped trying and was just there being nice. I could handle nice. It felt good having the niceness there especially from the cute boys.

I was still trying to play football with the boys in the neighborhood at twelve until I was hit in one of my titties by the ball. That's when I hung up my extracurricular activity playing football. Being a tom boy was slowly changing. I decided basketball would be my past time all the time. I loved playing basketball anyhow. Mostly alone so I could think and allow my imagination to take control. I lived in a fantasy world often. I was a dreamer. I was a free-spirited person. If I could fly I would have done so a million times and more. I loved myself even when circumstances said I shouldn't. But I was also a loaner. Some would say I was anti-social. Okay, sometimes I was anti-social, but I just looked at it as my time and my space was valuable and not everyone was allowed in my space.

I didn't have many friends. I was afraid of change and allowing people into my space, my life. I didn't want anyone abandoning me. I saw to many fake friends that my mom so called had. I observed people in our neighborhood stabbing each other in the back, fight one another and always talk about their so-called friends. I didn't need any friends like that. I didn't need no back stabbers as frineds.

My mom had a lot of crazy friends. They would come to our house and hang out with her, drinking and gossiping about the other women in the neighborhood. The kids would run around the house listening to the grown folks talk and humming the lyrics to the old school songs that we came to memorize we heard them so much. They all talked about each other. They talked a lot about men too. Who was sleeping with who. Who had good sex and who had the bigger package. Some things they said back then I had no idea what it meant, like drowning a man while having sex. Oh ok. Laughing out loud for real now that I know what that means

Sometimes my mom would go to her friend's house and hang out. They always had alcohol. It seems like the more alcohol, the more gossip and the more the kid's presence didn't matter.

One day we went over to one of my mom's friend's house, it was somewhere new with different people that I had never seen before. This time was no different and liquor was being consumed as usual. My mom's friend sent her daughter Melody over to the neighbor's house to get something. She asked if I could go with her and my mom let me. Melody was older than me. She was fourteen. I guess we were now friends. She seems to really like me and not judge me because of how I look or the fact that I was new in her neighborhood. I enjoyed being at her house and hanging out with her.

Everything was good until we got to her neighbor's house. There he was, the neighbor's son. He was sixteen years old, four years older than me and he was cute. His curls were sexy, his height was sexy. He didn't have on a shirt and his muscles were sexy. When he looked at me his eyes were sexy, and his smile was even sexy. I was for sure intrigued. Mesmerized by him being so sexy.

The girl I was with Melody, my new friend, picked up on me liking him instantly even when I tried to hide it. She knew him because he was her neighbor and she told him what I was thinking before I could even speak what I was thinking. I thought he was cute. I didn't know what that meant. Did that mean he had to be my boyfriend? I was nervous. I was scared. I wanted to get out of there fast. Then he told me I was cute. Wait, what? He thought I was cute too? He asked me to come to him. He said he didn't bite. I was so nervous to go but I did. My friend left me there with him. I wanted her to stay. She went into another room I guess to get what she was sent over there to get.

I walked over to him and the first thing he did was rub his hand on my face telling me how beautiful I was. He asked me how old I was and when I told him I was twelve he didn't believe me. He walked behind me and pulled me closer to him in an embrace. Then he touched my titties with both of his hands and said, "what twelve-year-old little girl has big titties like these. They soft too. All yours no tissue." He was really grabbing my titties, squeezing and caressing them. I couldn't move. I was afraid. I was confused.

He didn't even know me or my name and just started rubbing and caressing my titties. He was feeling me up with his hands on my body. He kept one hand on my titties holding me close to his body as he was behind me. "You like this, your nipples are hard," he said to me. Right then at that moment he took his other hand and shoved it in my pants inside my panties and touched my private parts. I couldn't make him stop. I didn't know how to make him stop.

I didn't know what to do at that moment but stand there and let him touch my titties and keep his hand in my panties like he was. I felt a new feeling that I had never felt before. My nipples got hard. He knew I must have liked it. I did like it, I think. He put his hand under my shirt and rubbed on my titties more and started kissing my neck as he moved his hand around in my panties and pressed his body up against mine firmly moving around. It felt good, like nothing I have ever felt before. This funny feeling was all over my body, weird but it felt good. Something was happening in my panties too. I wanted him to stop but I liked that feeling too. I didn't know what to do or if what I was feeling was wrong or right. I tried to wiggle out of his embrace because I was scared, and I didn't know if he would try to have sex with me. The kind of sex that those girls said would hurt. I didn't even know if what he was doing to me was considered sex.

Then he asked me the most frightening question ever. He asked me to be his girlfriend. Did that mean that he wanted to have sex with me right then? If I said yes would he make me?

I froze.

And then I was saved by Melody telling me we had to leave. She made him stop touching me and made him let me go. I should have had the strength to make him stop. I should have had the words to tell him to stop. I should have known better and made him stop. But I didn't. I couldn't. It felt good. It felt really good. I was weak in this unfamiliar place. I was scared, and I was experiencing something new, a boy that I thought was cute that was touching me without my permission that I couldn't find the words or actions to make stop. Nothing in my life's teaching prepared me for that moment.

I was so scared. Still I was scared. I had never let a boy touch me. They always snuck and touched my booty when I wasn't looking but nothing like this. Did he really want me to be his girlfriend or did he only ask me so he could have sex with me and do all those nasty things those girls said their boyfriend did to them or made them do? I wish I had someone who really knew the answers to tell me how I should feel and what I should do. I was lost and confused.

I left with Melody. I was glad she saved me. She didn't mention what she saw. I figured she knew that's what boys did, were supposed to do when they liked a girl. Then he came running up behind me and asked for my number. Said he wanted me to be his girlfriend. I told him I didn't even live over there, we were just visiting. He said we could just talk on the phone. I thought about it and figured talking on the phone was harmless, or at least should be. I wouldn't see him, so he wouldn't want me to have sex with him. I thought about it for a moment longer and then gave him my number, writing my name on the paper too. That was the first time ever that I gave a boy my number. I liked him. He was cute. He was sexy. He was more mature. He was my first boyfriend ever and I didn't have to have sex with him because I would never see him.

When we got back to my momma friend's house I was happy. I went to the bathroom because I felt wet. I hoped it wasn't my period but instead it was clear slimy stuff, lots of it. I didn't know what that was and forgot all about it when I came out of the bathroom. I was now being teased about having a boyfriend, but that tease felt good. I had a boyfriend and I felt like I had accomplished something. His voice was sexy too, so I could just fall in love with his voice. I guess I was ok with having a boyfriend. It wasn't so scary after all. Although, I didn't really know what it meant to have a boyfriend. I didn't know what the rules of a relationship would be.

Chapter 5
My New Boyfriend

When we got home I waited for the phone to ring. I was hoping he would call me as soon as we walked through the door. My mom was clueless to what happened at the neighbor's house. She sent me away out of her sight and I experienced a new feeling that I am sure I shouldn't have even known about at the age of twelve. I didn't know if she would be mad or not if she found out, but I didn't want her to find out either. She would whoop us for anything we did, even if we didn't even do it. If she thought we did something she would go off. Her temper was sometimes out of control. Sometimes we would say the wrong thing to her and get in trouble. When the phone rung I jumped up to check the caller ID and quickly answered the phone. It was him and I was too excited. I was trying to hide my excitement from him.

"Hello."

"Hi, may I speak to Ava?" he said in his sexy voice. I thought I was going to melt away. I almost hung up because I was so nervous, but I quickly remembered that he couldn't touch me on the phone.

"This is she." I answered back glad I didn't have to start the conversation. I was content with him leading.

"I thought it sounded like you. How long you been home?"

"We been home for about an hour now." I was guessing. It felt like several hours waiting for him to call me. But I definitely wasn't going to tell him that.

"For real? I was trying to give you time to get home before I called. I miss you already," he said to me and my mind went crazy. All I could do was smile because he said he missed me. I was happy that he missed me. I thought he must really like me to miss me already. I tried to think of what to say and couldn't, so I became a copycat.

"I miss you too." I didn't really miss him. I didn't even know him. Besides I just saw him earlier that day. I told him I missed him, but I didn't really mean it. Did he really mean it when he said it?

"I know you miss me. You miss me touching your titties don't you and playing with that pussy." Wait. What? What did he just say to me? Oh no. Since we are phone boyfriend and girlfriend's does that mean I have to talk about sex? I don't feel comfortable. I don't even know what to say. Maybe I need to rethink this boyfriend thing.

"No, I didn't tell you to touch me. You did it on your own," I said kind of loud. I had to make sure no one heard me. I took the phone dragging the long cord and went to my room and closed the door.

"You didn't stop me either. So, I know you liked it." He was cocky and sure of himself. "All girls like to be touched by their boyfriends." He was trying to explain to me I guess but I felt like he was telling me I was supposed to let him touch me and I was supposed to like it too.

"You were not my boyfriend when you touched me." That was the only thing I thought to say.

"Well am I your boyfriend now?" I guess he was nervous that I had changed my mind. He started talking in a sexy voice. "I really like you and I think you are the prettiest girl I have ever seen. You are beautiful Ava."

No one has ever told me I was pretty as much as he has all in one day. And then he said I was beautiful. I know it's the same but to me beautiful is prettier than pretty. "Yes, you are still my boyfriend," I said smiling. I liked him. He was cute.

"I am the luckiest man alive," he said in such an exciting loud voice.

"You are only sixteen you are not a man yet," I said. Surely I wasn't dating a man and he was really sixteen. I mean that is still too old probably, but he is under eighteen.

"Well I am not one of those immature boys you mess with. I am going to take care of you. I'm a hustler and I get money. You will see. You are going to be my main girl." Wait, what does main girl mean?

"What do you mean your main girl?"

"You know."

"I don't think I do know. I thought I was your girlfriend. Does that mean you will have other girlfriends too?" I guess I had an attitude or something because he sounded like he was nervous again and his smooth sexy talk changed a bit.

"Naw girl. I'm just playing with you. I wanted to see what you would say. You are my only girl, my only girlfriend."

I was still confused. I never had a boyfriend before. He talked sexy to me for about an hour and still managed to talk about sex more. When my momma made me get off the phone I laid on my bed thinking about him, hugging my favorite teddy bear. I noticed my panties were wet again like earlier. Then my mind started to wonder and remember the feel-good feeling he gave me earlier that day when he touched me. I got up and locked my bedroom door.

I was alone in my room after talking to my new boyfriend and I was feeling happy. I was curious still and I tried to create the same feeling he gave me. I got up under the covers on my bed and I started to caress my nipples with my own hands. It didn't feel as good as when he caressed them. Then I took my fingers and put them inside my panties like he did. I moved my fingers around in my panties like he did but the feelings were not the same. I even tried to rub my titties and move my fingers around in my panties at the same time closing my eyes and thinking about him, but it still didn't feel like it did when he had done it. I quickly forgot about how good it felt to have my nipples caressed. I dismissed the thoughts of wanting that feel good sensation back and I just enjoyed having a boyfriend that I only talked to on the phone.

I wasn't ready for sex. I didn't even want to have sex. Kids are only curious about things they are exposed to and have no idea how to do. Once that curiosity is either met or tried and failed, the curiosity most of the time disappears. I was back to my normal good girl self. I still had a boyfriend, but I was not about to have sex. I would be sure to wait until I was married to enjoy the feel-good feelings when I was ready and knew what I was doing.

Having a boyfriend was a new experience but so far it wasn't so bad. I was just glad I didn't have to see him and be in a situation again where he could touch me.

Chapter 6
Life as I knew

As the days passed, my life as I knew it went on. The excitement of having a boyfriend was slowly disappearing. It was back to school and doing what I was used to doing. Writing poetry in my room. Studying. Going to the basketball court to play ball. My new boyfriend called me every now and then, sometimes every day. One day I called his house and his mom answered and started yelling at me. It bothered me so much because I didn't like negative energy and I had it set in my mind that I was not calling him back. She said, "I'm tired of all these fast ass little girls calling here for my son. He out in the streets he ain't here." I didn't know what she meant by out in the streets, but I knew what she meant by girls being fast. I figured other girls were calling him to have sex. My feelings were hurt because sex equaled girlfriend, except in my case. I was not having sex any time soon. I would stay a good girl and save my sex for when I got older and found the man I would marry.

I still talked to him when he would call. I even questioned him about the other girls his mom said called him. This is when I found out what it meant when his mom said he was in the streets. "They know I sell drugs and get money in these streets and they want me because I got money… They my sister friends so that's how they got our number… I don't even like them girls I only love you…" So that's how he gets money. That's what it means to be in the streets. My boyfriend is a drug dealer. Oh shit! I didn't comment on anything he said. He sweet talked his way to my heart and I believed him I guess. I didn't know what I was supposed to think. I never see him, so I wouldn't know for myself. But I was still not calling his house anymore. His mom was not going to scream at me again.

We talked on the phone for months. He called me at all hours of the day. My mom would tell me, "some boy called you while you were at school. Why wasn't he at school." I would act like I didn't know who it was. He said my mom scared him that he didn't like it when she answered the phone. He started telling me what time he would call. I would unplug the phone down stairs, so my mom wouldn't hear the phone ring. Then he would tell me a time to call him so his mom wouldn't answer. If she did answer, I hung up quickly and waited for him to call me.

One night he called me he sounded different. He was still being sweet, but he sounded funny like something was wrong. He was so happy, or sleepy, or something. It was weird to me. He stopped talking about sex with me all the time because he knew I didn't like it. But this time he kept on talking about it.

"How long you gonna make me wait to have sex with you Ava?"

"You sound funny are you ok?"

"Yeah, I'm okay baby but you didn't answer my question. I love you and I want to make love to you. You the first girl that has ever made me wait."

The first? So, does that mean he has had sex with other girls? How many other girls? I mean he is only sixteen and he is not grown. I am sure only grown people are supposed to have sex. I think.

"How many girls are you having sex with?"

"What? I didn't say I been with other girls. I said I want to make love to you." Nope. He can't lie his way out of this one.

"Basically, you did. You said I was the first girl that has ever made you wait. And your mom did say a lot of girls were calling you. I am not stupid. If you are just say that you are." I managed to turn the conversation around and get the pressure off me, so I thought.

"Listen. Forget those other girls. I don't have sex with no one else. Not since we have been together. I want you to have my baby. Then I can get a real job, file taxes, claim the baby and get a lot of money. I can flip it with my business make us a whole lot more money. Then get us a place to stay. I can take care of all of us, you me and the baby." A baby? Really? He has gone from having sex to now getting me pregnant? I don't think having a boyfriend is in my near future.

"I am not having a baby. I have to go do something for my momma I will talk to you later." I lied.

"Wait please don't hang up. I just miss you and want to see you bad girl." There he goes with that sexy voice trying to sweet talk me again.

"You are just talking crazy to me."

"I'm sorry. I want to take you shopping, buy you some clothes and shoes. When can I take you shopping?" Shopping? I have never been shopping for anything new, I have always worn hand-me-downs.

"Shopping at the mall? How will we get there?" I did not want to be anywhere with him alone. He might try to touch my private parts again. Maybe if we go to the mall it will be ok.

"We can ride the bus or something girl let me figure that out. I am going to surprise you one day."

Moments later after talking on the phone a little while longer my mom came inside my room and took the phone out of my hands. She had the other phone and yelled into the receiver, "Boy you stay away from my daughter before I fuck you up. And don't call here anymore." Then she hung up.

I couldn't say anything to her, but I was mad that she hung up in his face. "Why you do that?"

"That boy is too old for you. Are you having sex with him? I am sure that's all he wants from you. I know your hot ass is having sex."

"Whatever. You don't know anything. You can't stop me from talking to him." I was furious. She didn't know how to talk calm to anyone. She always jumped to conclusions and reacted without knowing the story. I was a good girl. A virgin.

"I can, and I will keep you from talking to him." I could hear my boyfriend on the phone saying hello and calling my name. I guess he heard everything. My mom grabbed both phones and the cords and started screaming at everyone in the house. "I better not see anyone touch this phone. If it rings you better let it ring. I mean it. Ava, I will beat your ass if I find out you touched this phone."

And that was that. I guess my mom was keeping me from having a boyfriend. I was mad at first but relieved at the same time. Having a boyfriend was hard work. Even though all we did was talk on the phone. I am sure he will find another girlfriend soon. Especially after my mom screamed at him and threatened him. I wasn't going to have sex with him anyways, so I am sure it was only a matter of time before he ended our relationship. I went on with my life. I missed talking to him, I guess, but I knew I would be over it soon.

A few days later my mom was still guarding the phones. By then I just knew my boyfriend had moved on. My mom said she would hurt him if he didn't leave me alone. I stayed to myself as usual and wasn't really talking to her. She made me do a lot of chores and redo them if she thought I didn't do them good enough. At first, I was half way doing the chores, but after a couple days I started doing them correctly the first time. I guess it worked because she got off my case.

She allowed my siblings back on the phone but still watched me. I didn't talk to anyone else on the phone, so I never had the phone. I would go to the park and play basketball all day. It would be close to dark before I came home. I guess someone would tell my mom they saw me because she never said anything about me staying gone for so long.

It had been three weeks since I talked to my boyfriend. I accepted that he was my ex by then. I didn't even worry about the phone ringing unless my mom made me answer it and bring it to her. I stayed in my room mostly if I wasn't outside. I was a tom boy until I got titties.

After I realized I couldn't be tom-boyish I started trying to be more girly. One day my play uncle made his girlfriend do my hair and it was so pretty. She straightened it and curled it up in a flip. It stayed that way for two weeks. It didn't start curling back up until I had to walk in the rain. I will tell you about that soon.

School was out for spring break. It had been a month since I last talked to my boyfriend. He was now a memory and I never thought I would talk to him again let alone see him. I was outside on a Saturday afternoon, I had my basketball in my hand debating if I was going to the court or not. I threw the ball up against the side of the building over and over again, daydreaming, allowing my imagination to spark and take off until I heard someone call my name.

"Ava."

Chapter 7
My life changed forever

I was shocked. I was scared. I thought I should run as if he was a stranger. I didn't even know he knew where I lived. How did he know? Melody? My ex-boyfriend was standing in front of me. Well maybe he is still my boyfriend. I don't know. I am confused that he is here. "What are you doing here?"

"I wanted to see you." He was acting scared or something like he was hiding from someone. "Where is your mom?"

"She's in the house." He was scared of my mom.

"Come here girl give me a hug. I missed you so much." He walked over towards me. I was hesitant for a moment then I smiled and gave him a hug. But then he put his hand on my butt.

"What are you doing?" I said quickly jumping backwards from him. I looked at him with a puzzled look. I guess I had a moment of fear and it caused me to jump.

"I'm sorry I didn't mean to touch your butt. I am just so happy to see you and hold you in my arms. You are still my girlfriend right?"

"Are you still my boyfriend?" I wanted to know his answer before I gave mine.

"I love you, yes I'm still your boyfriend." Okay I guess I still have a boyfriend. I smiled.

"Okay. I guess I can try to sneak and call you again." He smiled at me and came over to hold my hands. I was actually excited to see him. I could tell he was scared my mom was going to come outside. Then my heart dropped.

"I came to get you, so we can go to the mall. I want to buy you some clothes and shoes." Then I was embarrassed by what I had on. My shoes were dirty and my clothes well they were hand-me-downs from someone else who had hand-me-downs.

"How are we going to get there? Did you drive here?"

"No, but we gone ride the bus to my uncle house, get his car, and then I can bring you right back." He didn't say anything about sex. Okay I guess that's ok.

"Okay we can go. I just can't be gone too long." I had to make sure I said that part so he would bring me right back.

He was excited. We walked to the bus stop, waited on the bus and headed for his uncle house. He had his arms around me the entire time. I was his girlfriend again and it felt good seeing him. I didn't know where we were, but I knew that we were far from my home. We walked from the bus stop to where he said his uncle lived. It was a duplex. Dogs were chained outside to trees barking. It was a scary place, but I felt safe because my boyfriend seemed to be familiar and assured me I was ok.

I didn't see a car in the driveway or anywhere close by, but he said he had a key and was going in to see where his uncle was. I was going to wait outside with the barking dogs, but he convinced me to come inside. Those dogs were big and acted like they wanted to eat me. So, I went inside and waited in the kitchen by the door because I was scared.

Scared to be in a stranger's house.

Scared to be in unfamiliar territory.

Scared to be alone with my boyfriend.

I was ready to go to the mall, get some clothes, shoes and get back home. I didn't hear anyone in the house talking. My boyfriend went in the back some where then after a few minutes came back with a box filled with some tennis shoes that were obviously worn. "Do you like these?" Why does he want to know if I like them? Are they his shoes?

"I guess they are all right. I mean I don't really know if a boy shoe is cute or not."

"They are girl shoes. Do you want these?" Wait a minute now. These shoes are clearly boy shoes and these shoes are clearly too big for me at least by 3 sizes. De`ja` Vu...

Did my feet look big or something? It reminded me for a second about the shoes in the foster care situation.

"They are boy shoes and no I don't want them. When are we leaving to go to the mall?"

"I'm waiting on my uncle he said he is on his way. Come in the living room with me."

"I'm good. I'm ready to go." I was really ready to go now. I guess that means we are here alone. "Who else is here?"

"My uncle and aunt are almost here. They don't like people in their kitchen so come on. Nothing is going to happen to you." Well I guess I can go with him. They are on their way home, so we should be good.

I walked into the living room with him and sat on the sofa. It was cluttered with stuff. "How long did they say they would be?" I was still inquiring because I was scared and uncomfortable. I had regret all over me. I should have not left my neighborhood with him. I should have lied and said I had something to do. Anything. Something.

"They almost here. You are so tensed relax won't you." I tried but I couldn't. I wanted to be at home. He sat down next to me. He put his arm around me. Then he started tickling me to make me laugh. I did laugh. It made me feel better. Next thing I know he kissed me. I have never kissed a boy before. Not how he was trying to kiss me.

When I pulled away he picked my light weight body up quickly and carried me inside a bedroom that was right beside the living room. I tried to sit up and move off the bed he placed me on, but he put his entire body on me.

"Just relax I'm just kissing you." I was not feeling this one bit. This was all wrong.

"I want to go home," I said, and fear was in every word I spoke.

"Not yet we still have to go shopping." Fuck shopping, I wanted to go home.

"I don't want to go shopping anymore I just want to go home." I was trying to be nice and get out of this situation.

"I will take you home after I make love to you." Fuck! I shouldn't have come. I want my momma, my daddy, my brother, his uncle, his aunt anyone to come save me.

"I didn't say we were having sex we were supposed to go shopping and take me home."

He kissed me all over my face and my neck. He held my upper body down with his strong upper body. His hands were on my pants unbuttoning them. "Let me up please. Stop, please stop." I didn't know what to do. He was hurting me. I couldn't think. He said his uncle would be there any minute, surely they will come save me. I quickly thought I needed to get away because they might not make it in time. He pinned my arms down so I couldn't stop him from taking my pants off. "Stop I have to pee. I have to use the bathroom."

"Ok go pee and take your clothes off while you are in there," he said to me letting me go one arm at a time easing up off me. "I love you girl. It will feel good I promise."

I couldn't say anything but give him a fake half smile trying to hold back my tears. I didn't want to have sex with him. I didn't love him anymore and he could not make love to me. I went into the bathroom and locked the door quickly. I figured I could stay in the bathroom until someone came home. Then I heard a knock at the door.

"You almost done?"

"No, go away." Was all I could think to say. I noticed there was another door on the other side of the bathroom. I only hoped it was a way out. I opened the door and it was connected to another room. I took off for the door to the bedroom hoping I could run out of the house. I didn't have on any shoes, but I didn't care I would walk all the way home bare footed if I had to. I ran towards the door and saw the door to the outside. I tried to hurry hoping he didn't hear me and there he was.

He grabbed me. He picked me up and carried me back into the bedroom and threw me on the bed. "You playing games. I see I'm gon have to take this pussy." He held me down with all his strength.

"Stop. Please no I don't want to." He was trying to get my pants off to have sex with me. Somebody help me.

"Stop fighting me girl." He screamed. He put one hand around my neck when I kicked him with my knee in the nuts trying to get away. He quickly let my neck go when he realized he was chocking me. He used his head, his arms, his chest to hold my body down trying to get me to stop fighting him. His fingers were digging into my skin. It hurt. I needed to get away but he was too strong.

"You can't do this please stop. You are hurting me." I was crying. I was pleading for him to stop. He was hurting me. My wrist, my neck, my chest, my arms, my thighs. He was hurting me. He had his entire upper body holding me down and used one hand to take off my pants. He raised up briefly to jerk my pants off my feet and when I tried to get up he pushed me back down to the bed and covered my entire body with his holding me down. My tears did not faze him. He didn't care that I was crying or that he was hurting me. I tried to keep my legs closed and he forced them open. His fingers were digging into my thighs to pull my legs apart. He was hurting me. No one was there to save me. He forced his penis inside me and I screamed an excruciating cry. He covered my mouth with his hand. I begged him to stop but he didn't. He kept on going. My tears meant nothing to him. I don't want a boyfriend ever again. Why would anyone want a boyfriend? This was the worse day of my life. I was hurting, I was in pain. He didn't give a damn, no one gave a damn and no one came to save me.

Those few moments felt like an eternity of pain. When he was done he laid on top of me for a few moments. "I love you girl. Sorry if I hurt you. This was the best pussy I have ever had. You will always be my beautiful girlfriend."

I didn't respond to him I couldn't respond to him. When he got up off of me he looked at the bloody mess on the sheets and all over him. He looked up at me and said, "You were a virgin?"

I rolled my eyes at him. "Can I have a rag to wash myself up?" I wanted to get my clothes back on fast. I picked each piece up off the floor holding them to my body to cover up.

"My baby was a virgin. I was your first." He got up coming towards me holding me in his arms rocking and kissing my face.

"Can I have a rag please? I have to get home before I get in trouble." I wanted to get home quick.

He gave me a rag and I closed myself in the bathroom. I cried, and I couldn't stop crying. I felt like I was beat up. I had bruises on my neck. All over my arms. On my chest. On my side. On the inside of my thighs and down my legs. I washed up and I was still bleeding. Is it because I was a virgin? Is it because he forced himself inside me? I am bleeding a lot. I washed good and put my clothes back on.

"Baby you ready?" I heard him through the door.

I opened the door. "Can we go now? Where is your uncle?"

"My uncle won't be here until later. We can go to the mall another time. I have a bus schedule let me look when the next bus come." He opened the bus schedule and it was another thirty minutes before the bus would come. "We can wait here until it comes."

"I want to wait at the bus stop so we don't miss the bus." I wanted to get out of their quick. I wanted my pillow and my bed so I could cry. I wanted to tell my momma what happened so she could comfort me. I wanted my life back and the pain to go away.

"Ok come on. You sure you don't want those shoes?"

No, I don't want those ugly ass shoes. I can't fit them big boats. They are boy shoes. I was screaming those words in my head but I simply told him, "No." We walked to the bus stop and waited for what seem like forever for the bus to come. He gave me money for the bus fair and said he will see me later. Wait. You are not going with me? I didn't protest but I was scared to be by myself. He already took my sex and now he was pushing me away to be alone.

I got on the bus by myself. I wanted to cry but there were people all around me.

I felt wetness in between my legs.

I was hurting emotionally.

I was hurting physically.

I felt like everyone was looking at me and I wanted no one to see me.

I don't know what just happened but why did it have to happen to me. I said no, I told him to stop. Why didn't he stop? Is this what boyfriends do to their girlfriends? I should have just had sex with him and not fight him. Was it my fault? I should have stayed home. I should have ran from him the first day I met him. I should have never given him my phone number. Tears were seeping out of my eyes. I tried to wipe them before they fell but couldn't. I was crying inside, and it was pushing the tears out beyond my control.

I rode the bus alone all the way home. I had to walk about three blocks to get to my house. As I was approaching my house I saw a crowd around my porch. I heard someone say, "There goes Ava right there." Then everyone started talking and my mom started screaming at me...

Chapter 8

My side of the story untold

"I am going to beat the hell out of you. You left in a car full of boys. Six boys at that. Your hot ass is grounded for life. Where have you been with them damn boys?" She was screaming loud enough so everyone could hear and acting so irate so everyone could see her as if she was putting on a show for them.

"I wasn't in a car and I wasn't with six boys." I wanted to tell her what happened to me. Why are all of these people at my house? They were all quiet.

"Mary saw you. She has no reason to lie." What? But it was a lie. I looked Mary in the eyes and she stepped back. I guess she didn't think my mom would tell on her. She lied on me. She knew she was lying too. Before I could say anything else my mom took the belt she had in her hand and swung it across my face. I screamed out in pain. She paused just briefly realizing she hit me in my face. Everyone around us was ohhing and commenting. Some were even laughing. Her friends were there. Some of the kids that lived in the neighborhood were there. My siblings were there. Then my momma started swinging the belt repeatedly. I was trying to run in the house and she was trying to pull me back to keep me outside so she could keep whooping me in front of everyone. What was she trying to prove? I am her child.

"Momma stop!" I cried. "Momma please stop!" I wanted her to hold me. I wanted her to rock me. I wanted her to listen to me. For once in her life I wanted her to love her daughter and I wanted to feel her love. I needed to feel her love. Instead she beat me with that belt. If she only knew what just happened to me maybe she would stop. But she didn't. I tried to get away. She pulled my hair when I tried to go up the steps. She pulled my leg making me fall back down the steps. She swung that belt so many times. I think I went numb.

Did she hate me?

More pain. More hurt. More abuse.

All in one day.

I made it to my room. She busted through the door still screaming calling me bitches and whores. I could hear the neighbors outside laughing. It fed her anger. She didn't know what happened. I wish she did. She kept whooping me with that belt. She didn't care where it landed on my body. I tried to hide beside my bed in the corner. She was still hitting me. I was screaming for her to stop. I tried to get under my bed but she moved the bed out of the way.

She finally stopped. I didn't hear any more laughs. I didn't hear any more talking. She left my room and slammed my door close telling me to stay in my room and don't come out. After that, I couldn't hear anything but my sobs, my sniffles and the sound of my broken heart shattering into a million more pieces. I stayed in my room. I didn't come out for anything. I didn't even eat anything that day. I wanted to be left alone.

It was late at night and I heard my little sister tapping at my door. She said she made me something to eat. I wasn't answering her.

"Ava, I am sorry momma hurt you. I know you're not ok. I made you some food. Shut up I don't care she my sister." I heard her saying. I guess she was talking to one of my brothers. "I made you something to eat Ava." She slid some crackers and cheese under the door. The crack was big enough. She put them on a piece of paper and slid them easily under the door. I was sitting on the floor of my closet not saying a word. I was numb. My body hurt. "Ava please talk to me so I know you are ok in there."

"Go away. Please go away and leave me alone." I didn't want to ignore her. I knew she was hurting. I was her big sister. I slept in my closet that night. I woke up early the next morning and realized my favorite blue pants were ruined. Blood was everywhere from my private parts and from some of the whips I had from being whooped. I changed my clothes and hid my pants. I went into the bathroom to pee and wash the dried-up blood off me. My body hurt so bad. I had bruises all over me from the forceful evasion of sex to my body. Then I had whips all over me including my face from the beating I endured from the one person I thought would protect me

I went back in my room locked the door and laid back in my closet. I didn't come out of my room all day. That night my sister was outside the door talking again and she put her fingers under the door. I saw them. She hadn't seen me in two days, so I went over and touched her fingers and she jerked them back. She was scared and jerked her hand back quickly, but she was excited at the same time. I couldn't tell her my pain. She was young and innocent. I couldn't let her comfort me because that was not the comfort I craved. All I could do was lay in my closet holding on to my pillow.

I didn't talk.

I didn't think.

I didn't use my imagination to escape.

I didn't do anything but hurt and sometimes cry.

I stayed in my room for three days straight. I would drink water out of the bathroom sink when I went to pee. My face was puffy, eyes were puffy, and the marks were still there on my face and my body. The bruises were still on my neck and everywhere else. The visible parts that hurt would heal quickly but the inner hurt, well that's an entire different story.

Chapter 9
My life was not the same

After about a week my face looked better. The bruises however were turning all kinds of colors and were still visible. My thighs were the worse. I guess from fighting so hard not to allow him to enter me. I wasn't strong enough. He was stronger. My sister and brothers were bringing me food. I didn't want to see my mother. I still didn't want to talk about what happened, but my sister would come in my room with me even if I didn't say anything to her. No matter what I know my siblings had my back and would never intentionally hurt me. I didn't want to go outside because I didn't want people making fun of me. My friends would come to see if I could come out, but I never did. I don't know how long I was grounded but I didn't want to do anything anyhow. I would stay in my room listening to music and writing poetry.

> You said you loved me
>
> I thought it was true
>
> But you hurt me
>
> I didn't know what to do.
>
> Why didn't you stop
>
> I told you no
>
> Instead you held me down
>
> You wouldn't let me go
>
> I cried out loud
>
> You hurt me so bad
>
> You as my boyfriend
>
> I wish I never had
>
> I never thought
>
> That's how my first time would be
>
> I am so confused
>
> What does that mean for you and me

Poetry was an escape for me. Expressions of my feelings. I loved to write. After a few days of doing nothing I went back to my writing to escape. I eventually ventured out of my room.

My mom was being sarcastic. "You finally came out of that room I see. I thought I killed you, but I see you will live."

I still wasn't talking to her. I wouldn't stay in her presence long. I know she could see the bruises on my arms and neck. I had on a t-shirt. It was hot. They were going away but you could still tell they were there. She probably thought she did them all. I would be glad when they went away completely. I wasn't going back outside until they did.

When I finally went back outside my friends never brought up what my mom did. They only asked if I was ok. A few kids were being mean when they saw me, but I just ignored them. I went to see Mary and asked her why she lied on me. She was scared when she first saw me. I guess she thought I was going to try to fight her. I didn't have any fight left in me. I just wanted to know why she lied and what made my momma look for me on that particular day when she never had before.

"I didn't tell your mom that, I told her I saw someone that looked like you walking towards a grey car but I didn't think it was you. She was looking for you after your neighbor across from you told your mom she saw you talking to a boy then leave with him."

"Ok." I guess I got my answer. That explained why she started to look for me.

"Are you okay? I didn't think that was right what she did to you."

"No, I am not alright. I was wondering, all those people that were outside, all those adults and no one tried to stop her. Why didn't you stop her?" It just hit me that no one tried to help me when I was being beat by my mother.

"Well I uhm, I, she was pretty mad. I didn't want her going off on me."

"I will see you later." I didn't want to talk about it anymore. It actually made me mad when I thought about no one helping me. No one seems to ever help me. I am living in someone else's world.

My mom wasn't there for me.

My dad has never been there for me.

My boyfriend wasn't there for me.

Everyone seemed to want to hurt me in some form or fashion. Even the perverts in the neighborhood see me and want to take advantage of me. Girls want to fight me because I am pretty, and the men want to have sex with me because I was pretty. Why does being pretty feel so much like a damn curse. At times I wish I was invisible. I was beautiful, but nothing was easy. At least it seemed that way. My beauty was supposed to be a blessing but seemed to instead be my curse.

I was holding on to hurt but didn't realize to what extent. It was building up inside of me and I didn't have a release button. I didn't know how to release any of it. I didn't even know right from wrong, even when it felt so wrong. I kept everything bottled up inside and went on with my life.

School started back and one day I was walking home with a few friends when my boyfriend came from out of nowhere. I don't even know if I should be calling him my boyfriend. It had been at least a month since I saw him, since that awful day he hurt me.

"What are you doing here?" I asked not excited to see him. I was good if I never saw him again.

"I came by your house every day to see you. One of your friends told me what happened. I wanted to make sure you were ok. Can I walk you home please? Just me and you?" They told you what happened, what about what you did? Did you tell them that? I wanted to scream my words to him, but nothing came out.

"I will catch you later Ava." My friend said and walked on with the rest of the girls.

"See you later," I said as she walked away. "I guess you can walk with me." I didn't know what else to say to him. I wondered if he really came by my house. And what for.

"I wanted to make sure you were ok. Sorry if I hurt you." Sorry? Did he just say sorry? I was filling up with rage.

"Why did you hurt me?" I blurted out. He was startled. Tears were welling up in my eyes.

"I didn't know you were a virgin."

"Why does that matter? You still didn't have to hurt me. I wasn't ready to have sex."

"I'm sorry, you are right I should have stopped. My sister said it's always hard for girls when it's their first time. You are not like them other girls. Are you mad at me?" Other girls? I knew he was talking about the fast girls his mom said calls him at home.

"Yes." I was mad. But the free-spirited person wanted to let it all go. But that moment changed my life. I couldn't get my innocence back. I couldn't erase the memories of hurt and pain. I couldn't relive my first time to make it better. I couldn't save my first sex for marriage. I didn't have my innocence anymore because he took it from me. And that's something I would have to live with the rest of my life. He did that to me. Of course, I am mad. But as a kid I didn't realize just how mad I should have been.

"I bought you something." He reached inside his pocket and pulled out a necklace that had a heart on it. "I love you and I still want you to be my girlfriend." He put his arms around my neck to put the necklace on me.

"How do you know I even want this?" I was being stubborn. How could he hurt me then be so nice to me?

"You my girl. I want you to have nice things. I won't hurt you again I promise. Next time we have sex it won't hurt like last time."

"Who said it will be a next time?" Sex again? No thank you. I was never going to be alone with him again.

"Ok. We will take it slow then, and only when you are ready."

And just like that, he said he was sorry and didn't mean to hurt me. I just pushed what happened into the back of my mind. That's what happens when you have a boyfriend. I was supposed to give him sex. At least that is what the girls at school say. If you don't give them sex they will take it and hurt you. I didn't know any better. I didn't know that what he did to me was wrong and I didn't know that no really meant no. Stop really meant stop. Tears, screams and fighting really meant that the action against me was unwanted. I didn't know that what he did to me was rape!

It was acceptable in my mind because I didn't know. My mom never talked to me about how I was supposed to be treated. She never showed me what real love felt like. My father was never there to tell me how he would break a boy's neck for hurting his daughter. My father wasn't there to tell me about boys, how they are, what to do and not to do, what to accept and not to accept. My learning took place from what I saw around me, what I heard about in school, and now by what I experienced.

He met me at school a few times but would never walk me all the way home. I guess he didn't go to school. He was always waiting on me when I got out of school. He eventually stopped coming so much.

My mom let me get my hair done for the first time only because my play uncle heard about what happened to me and he wanted me to feel better about myself. He knew that women felt better about who they were when they looked better. I thought I was fine. I didn't have any style really and wore my hair in a ponytail most days. I will admit I was tender headed and barely combed the kinks out of my hair. So I guess that's why he started with my hair. He got his girl to do my hair at his house. He told her to make my hair beautiful just as I was beautiful. My dad wasn't in my life so that felt good to hear a father figure say that about me. My hair was beautiful. It was straightened, no kinks, and curled outward in layers. I felt like a superstar. But I don't think my mom liked it. I think it may have been too pretty. It made me want to dress prettier. And that's when I started feeling more girly.

One day soon after, my mom and I had a fight. I swear I felt like she hated me and she always made me feel like she was jealous of me. I left home. I guess it was called running away. I went up to Mary's house. No one knew I was there. When I was there I called my boyfriend and he answered on the first ring. I figured he was already on the phone he answered so quickly. I told him what happened and where I was staying. He wanted to come see me. I thought it was ok. So he came over to her house to see me. He got there quick. When he arrived, I was sitting on the porch outside. Mary lived on the second level. I forgave her for lying on me. I didn't know whose truth to believe no how. I saw him when he pulled up. Someone was in the car with him and they stayed there when he came up to see me. "Hey," I yelled down letting him know I was up there.

"There go my baby," he said smiling up at me. He ran up the steps and came over to give me a hug.

"Is your friend going to wait in the car for you?" I asked wondering.

"Yeah he's not going anywhere until I am ready." Okay I thought.

We sat outside for a while. Mary said he could come inside with me, that it was ok. I was hesitant but he got up first so I followed. We sat in the living room talking and he had his arms around me holding me. When I got up to pee he said he would be right back, that he was going to the car to check on his friend. When I came back to the living room I heard him outside on the porch talking to

Mary. I couldn't figure out what they were saying but I saw him give her something. I figured it was some drugs that he sold. She did smoke weed. Maybe that's what it was. When he came back inside he closed the door and locked it. "Why you close the door? Mary is out there." She was outside with her friend sitting in the place where me and my boyfriend were sitting before.

"She said she would be right back. She was giving us some alone time." What? Shit!

"Where did she go?" I wanted to know how long she was going to be gone. Why would she leave me alone anyways?

"Come on let's go to the back." I didn't want to have sex with him again. I didn't want him to hurt me either. I was scared all over again. "I am not going to hurt you. You can take control and go slow it won't hurt if you are on top." Damn. He did want sex. His eyes were red and he seemed like he was high or something. He pulled my hand pulling me up from the sofa holding on to me tight and I followed him to the back room.

I looked out the window as we passed it and saw that the car he came in was now gone. "Where did your friend go? Did he leave you?"

"I told him I would call when I was ready to go. He will come back and get me." He undressed me slowly caressing my body. I just stood there and let him. I didn't want to fight him again and have a repeat of last time. "Don't be scared. I will talk you through it and you can go as slow as you want to." My heart was beating so fast you could see it through my clothes.

Okay I guess. He pulled me on top of him and he laid back on the bed. I didn't know what I was doing. He talked me through it. "It's not going in." I told him. I was so afraid it was going to hurt me again.

"You have to sit down on it. You are not pushing it in." He then grabbed my hips and pulled me down on him.

"Ouch. Stop you said I could take control." He kept pushing himself in and out of me going in further and further. I was tense, and I wanted this to be over.

"It's almost all the way in," he said to me still pulling my hips down and pushing his hips up.

"Okay," I said in a fearful way. It was so uncomfortable for me. He eventually got it all the way inside and held my hips down on him so I couldn't pull up.

"Rock your hips back and forth. Don't raise up just move back and forth." I did what he said. I was trying not to be so tense. I was scared it was going to hurt really bad like before. After a few moments of rocking back and forth I felt something. It was all over my body and I was starting to like the rocking feeling. I was panting. Then I felt a gush of wetness between my legs and I thought I came on my period.

"I feel wet down there." I didn't want to tell him I thought I was bleeding.

"You just had an orgasm baby," he said to me smiling. He flipped me over on my back. He had sex with me for a very long time as I lay on my back. That was the only way he could go fast. I was scared to go fast by myself. I was feeling good with him kissing me and touching me like when I first met him. I guess having sex with your boyfriend wasn't too bad. I shouldn't have fought him last time. I should have just let him do what he wanted to do like now. After all he was my boyfriend right? That's what I was supposed to do, let him have sex with me. Right?

Is that right?

How do I know for sure if what I have been taught to be right is really wrong?

It feels wrong.

But he was my boyfriend and the rules in the hood said that's what I was supposed to do, that's what he was supposed to do. Right?

I never heard Mary come in. I don't know if she did or not. My boyfriend didn't call his friend to come back and get him. He ended up spending the night at Mary's house with me. After he was done having sex with me he passed out. I laid down beside him and he put his arms around me and held me all night. He woke up early the next morning. He had sex with me again. This time it wasn't gentle like the night before. It seemed like he was in a rush. When he was done he called his friend to come pick him up and he quickly dressed to leave. His friend must have been close because as soon as he was dressed his friend was outside. I walked outside with him. He gave me one hundred dollars told me to buy me some new shoes. He didn't like my old dirty ones. He said his girl should have new shoes. I never had this much money before. He made me go back inside and lock the door before he left. I watched out the window as he got in the car and drove away.

I guess that was ok. It didn't hurt like last time and I didn't have any bruises. He even gave me money. I was thirteen now, so I was getting older. The next day he wanted me to come see him. I guess he liked having sex with me.

Chapter 10
Why me

I had to ride the bus over to his house. I didn't go to his house though, I was supposed to meet him at the bus stop. I didn't know where I was. I got off the bus where he told me to. It looked kind of familiar, but I wasn't sure. I waited for at least thirty minutes before I finally started walking around. I didn't have access to a phone to call him. Then I saw him standing close to a car and handing the guy inside something. I walked over towards him. "I have been waiting on you," I said, and he looked up.

He started looking around. What was that for? "I was coming. How long you been off the bus?"

"At least thirty minutes." It was longer than that. I was guessing because I didn't have a watch, but I knew it was longer. "You don't seem excited to see me." He didn't. Then he started to smile.

"Girl yes I'm excited to see you. Your hair still looks pretty. Come here give me a hug." He wrapped his arms around me. It felt good to have affection from man. He was a man to me anyhow. He was tall and strong. He was mature and had money. He did what he wanted to do. "We are going to go to my house for a minute okay. You can meet my sisters, they can see how pretty you are." Oh!

I was so nervous meeting anyone in his family. What if they didn't like me? What if his mom is there? I had sex with her son. She is going to call me a fast ass hot momma to my face this time. I am so scared. "Is your mom going to be there?"

"Is that why you are squeezing my hand so tight?" He said looking down at me. Scared was written all over my face. "My mom will like you, don't be scared. But she is not even there, just my sisters."

Okay I can deal with meeting his sisters. I talked to one on the phone before. She was nice she asked me if I liked her brother. I hope she is there. "Ok. What else are we doing?"

"My aunt and uncle are having a cookout at their place. We will go down there for a little bit." Oh no, not back there I don't want to go back to the same place where it happened. I was panicking, and I guess I was squeezing his hand harder. It's like he knew what I was thinking. "It's a different aunt and uncle from where we were the first time, you know. You are really scared. I am going to need a new hand, you are squeezing so hard. Come here girl."

He let go of my hand and put his arm around my neck still looking around I was assuming he didn't want someone else to see him. I wasn't sure. "Why do you keep looking around?" I couldn't help but to ask.

"Oh, I have to watch my back out here in these streets. These niggas try to run up on you when you are not expecting it and take your shit."

"Oh," I said and held on tight.

"Nothing is going to happen to you girl. Relax, stop being so tense. You are safe with me ok." After those words I guess I was relaxed. "My sisters are going to love you. They may ask you a lot of questions though. I am their only brother." He started playing with my hair. I pulled away and smiled. I knew he must have really liked my hair.

"Yeah I remember you saying that. It's ok." There we were at his backdoor, seconds before walking in to meet his family and be bombarded with questions.

"Hey what you doing home? Who is that Ava?" His sister said to him looking at me. But how did she know it was me?

"Yeah this is Ava. My girlfriend," he said holding my hand then pulling me closer to him to kiss my cheek.

"Hello." I was so nervous.

"She is beautiful. I can see why you like her so much." His sister said he liked me. That must be a good sign, right?

"Where you from? You look scared and don't look like no west side girl." His older sister said.

"She not from out here she lives out east." My boyfriend spoke up. I was ok with him talking for me.

His baby sister or his sister's child came up to me and hugged my leg. "You pretty," she said in a sweet little voice.

"Yeah she is pretty. I don't know what she sees in your ugly ass." his sister said to him, jokingly. She was a couple years older than him and they all seemed to love their brother dearly.

"Whatever, I look good. You just mad you didn't get the cuteness I got." He shot back.

"You got me messed up. Cute is all that I am. You better ask these niggas riding my coat tail paying my bills." She shot back. I think the little girl is her daughter. She called her momma. She was young to have a baby. He told me to sit on the couch and he ran upstairs. The sisters asked me some questions but not too many before he came back down stairs.

"Come up here to my room Ava," he said. I quickly looked up at his sisters.

"You know if momma catches you up stairs with a girl, you will be in trouble." His sister said.

"I am not going to be up here long. Come on Ava." I followed him upstairs.

"When is your mom coming?" I asked nervous that she would catch me in his room.

"She at work she won't be home for a while. We will be gone by that time."

"Are we still going to the cookout?" I didn't know what he was planning once we got upstairs but I was hoping we would go somewhere fun and he didn't want to just have sex with me again.

"Yes, we are going. I want to feel you before we go." Feel me?

"What does that mean?" He didn't answer me. I guess I sounded irritated.

"Come here girl," he said pulling me close to his body. He locked my fingers inside his and pulled them behind my back with his as he started to kiss my neck. He walked backwards towards the wall pinning me against it. I could feel his penis through his pants pressing up against my stomach. He reached up and turned the light off.

"It's dark in here I can't see anything." It was pitch black. I know there were windows in the room, but I think the curtains shielded the sunlight from coming through. I couldn't see him, I could only feel him touching me.

"I got you. We don't need to see anything. Let me explore your body in the dark." And there I was having sex with him again in his bedroom at his momma house.

After he was done, and I put my clothes back on I realized I had a big hinky on my neck. My momma is gonna kill me. Wait. I forgot I ran away from home. I don't have to go home. I can do what I want to do. "Are we staying here?" I asked watching him put on his shoes that looked brand new.

"My mom will be home soon. We going to my aunt house and then we will come back later."

"Ok." I guess I was ok. I was a long way from home and all I had to hold on to was my boyfriend. As long as he would be close by me I would be ok.

We arrived at his aunt house and it was a lot of people there. Music was loud, people was drinking, and smoking weed, and the grill was smoking some good smelling meat. Little kids were running around everywhere and some of the girls were having a dancing contest in the middle of the yard. This looked like one big happy family affair. I walked into the house with my boyfriend. I sat down stairs for a while and even ate some good food.

After, my boyfriend's uncle called him upstairs and I didn't want to stay by myself so I went with him. His uncle was scary looking, but he seemed to be cool. He said we could stay in his room and watch tv, me and my boyfriend. I was thinking cool, I can handle that. I sat down on the edge of the bed in his room. This room was weird, it had bunk beds surely this was not his uncle's room. Next thing I know the uncle called my boyfriend into the hall way. Hesitant, my boyfriend met him in the hall way. After a few words exchanged quietly, the uncle came into the room shutting and locking the door behind him. My boyfriend stood there in the hallway, didn't move. He didn't try to follow his uncle into the room. He stood there frozen, looking.

The door locked, I was confused. The uncle walked over to me where I was now standing beside the bed. I tried to walk around him to leave and he grabbed me. One hand on my butt and the other on my back. "Let me go." I yelled pushing him backwards off me.

"Come on baby. Let me make you feel good. I can do things no little young boy can do," he said trying to hold on to me tighter.

"Let me go, I am going to scream," I said still trying to push him off me. I heard some taps at the door and could hear a low voice calling "unc" and I knew it was my boyfriend. Why did he let him come in here and do this to me? Why wasn't he in here trying to save me? Why is this happening to me? "Let me go now," I said as loud as I could.

"Shut your pretty ass up and let me fuck you." He pushed me backwards down on the bed.

My mind was racing, the knocks stopped. No one was coming to save me. He was unbuckling his belt on his pants. This grown ass man was about to take my sex and hurt me.

I started screaming as I stood to my feet and tried to run pass him. He grabbed me with one hand holding his pants up with the other. I don't know where I got the strength from but I grabbed his shoulders (he was short) and with all my might I raised my knee and rammed it into his crotch.

He immediately let me go screaming, "you bitch." I ran passed him and when he tried to catch me while still bent over I pushed his tv over onto him. He must have loved that tv. It must have been the only one he had. He saved that tv and I was able to unlock the door and run out.

My boyfriend was standing there looking stupid. Why didn't he kick the door down? Go get help. Is this what men did? Is this what boyfriends do? I hated him right then. I wanted to run home, anywhere besides there. I ran down the steps with my boyfriend on my heels. "Did he hurt you? What happened?" He was trying to talk to me and I kept on moving out the door. I could hear his aunts and other people in the house and outside asking "What happened to her? What ya'll do to that pretty girl? Was it your uncle? That crazy mother fucker. Ya'll know he crazy. You take care of that girl. Something bad must have happened."

All these grown folks in the house and no one checked on me. I was a kid. I might not have looked like a kid, but I was a kid. I was hurting inside. Why did men want to touch me in my private parts? Is my beauty really a curse? That's what I feel like a beautiful damn curse. I didn't ask for this. God made me this way. But why does this man think he can have me? I didn't tell him he could. I want to be back in my room with the door closed, writing poetry, listening to music, drowning all of this out. I want to be safe.

It was drizzling outside but I didn't care one bit. I loved the rain. It was soothing. But it was a little chilly. My hair was getting wet. It probably wouldn't look the same. My boyfriend caught up with me telling me to wait. Made up some bull crap story saying his uncle said he wanted to see if I was loyal to his nephew. And that's why he didn't "break the door down" and come save me. I don't know if he was telling the truth or not but either way I wanted to go home right then. I wasn't feeling having a boyfriend anymore. I wasn't feeling being away from home. I wished my mom would save me. Did she even care that I wasn't home? My father sure as hell didn't give a damn, never had. Maybe if he was in my life I would know what was right and what was wrong when it came to boys, men, unwanted touches, molestation, abuse, rape!

My boyfriend wrapped his arms around me and held on to me tight. I closed my arms feeling a bit of relief and it quickly diminished when I saw his uncle walking towards us. I pushed back. "Here comes your uncle." I was scared.

"Stay right here, I will be back. He is not going to hurt you." I stood there and waited, keeping my eyes on his uncle. I couldn't hear what they were saying because they were so far away from me. His uncle walked back towards the house and my boyfriend ran back over to me. "Ava, he is going to take you home," he said. Really?

"I am not getting in the car with him. I will walk home first." I shot back. Is he crazy? Surely he didn't think I was getting in the car with this man by myself.

"I will be with you, it will be ok. I told him he was wrong for doing that. He said he was sorry. It's raining you don't need to be walking nowhere." Sorry. Here we go with this fix all word again. Does sorry supposed to always make shit better? Is sorry really a fix all word? Was anyone who said they were sorry really sorry? Why do something bad just to try and fix it with "I'm sorry?" Is that the way it is or supposed to be? Sorry? Yeah, he is sorry alright. A sorry excuse for a damn man. Rain or no rain I knew I would probably be better off walking home no matter how long it took. But I was a scared little girl and wanted someone to come save me.

"If you are with me I guess its ok. I am just ready to go home. I am not having fun anymore." I was sad. He knew I was sad. I was irritated. He knew I was irritated. I was hurting inside. He had no clue how bad. I was also a scared girl not knowing where I was or which way to turn.

"I am sorry I really am. I will get you home. My uncle is crazy. I mean he really crazy," he said emphasizing crazy. That should have been my clue, but I didn't know how to look for clues. I was still accepting that he was taking me home.

His uncle came out of the house with keys in his hand and a little teacup dog in his other hand. What grown man has a little bitty dog like that? My boyfriend was going to sit in the back with me, but his uncle made him get in the front seat. It was a two-door car and I had to climb behind the seat into the back. We all got in the car and I sat right behind my boyfriend. His uncle turned the music all the way up as loud as he could. The music was way too loud. He threw his little dog in the back seat right into my lap. I know he did that on purpose. The dog squealed and went to the other side of the car to lie down. I couldn't wait to get home and far away from him. This man was showing all of his crazy colors.

He kept whispering to my boyfriend. I couldn't hear anything over that loud ass music. I really wished his speakers would blow. We were approaching a red light and I looked up into the front seat and the uncle pulled out a gun and placed it in his lap. He had one hand on the gun and one hand on the steering wheel and he kept looking at my boyfriend saying something. He looked pissed. I was scared. I was shaking. I wanted to be anywhere else besides there right now.

He stopped at the red light. Cars were all around us. My boyfriend opened the door and stepped one foot out. His uncle pushed him and he stood to his feet. I leaned my head out noticing he was saying something and I asked are we getting out. He was motioning me with his eyes to get out. It all happened so fast. It all felt so unreal. I couldn't believe the situation I was in, all at the sake of having a damn boyfriend. My mind went blank. The noise stopped. I was in tunnel vision mode and nothing in the world made sense to me at that moment but staying alive.

My heart beating fast was all I could hear at that moment besides the windshield wipers swishing and the screeching of tires as the car sped off. The door was still open, and my boyfriend was still standing in the middle of the street, in the rain. There was about a half foot opening from the back seat to get out of the car. I don't know how, actually I do know now, but my entire body lunged from the back seat of the car and I rolled into the middle of the wet street. The rain was coming down. My hair, my clothes, I was soak and wet. The rain hitting my skin was cold but soothing. It had to be God lifting my numb body out of that car. I felt safer out of the car than I did inside the car with him all alone.

After rolling in the street I got up so fast and ran to the sidewalk. I was crying. I was running. I was scared. Tears were falling from my eyes and the rain was washing them from my face. I never felt so alone in my life, more so than I did at that moment. But somehow, I knew someone had me. I was crying so hard and so loud. I started walking. I could see people riding by slow to look at me, thinking I would be covered in scraps and blood.

People were yelling out their windows asking if I was ok. A car full of ladies pulled up next to me, "Baby girl are you ok. Can we take you home? You are too pretty to be out here like this. You could have been hurt really bad. Come on let us take you home."

I thought about it for a second to let them take me home. I mean they sounded more concerned about my wellbeing than anyone in my life has ever sounded. At that moment I felt hands wrap around my shoulders and hug me. My boyfriend had caught up to me. "She's ok. I got her," he said to the ladies.

"Fuck him. He probably got you into this mess. You didn't have her when she was jumping out that damn car. Come on get in the car with us baby girl. We will take you home. I promise." I promise. I promise. I promise. Those words echoed in my head. I felt like I could trust these ladies. But yet, I didn't know them either. I didn't know the uncle and I got in the car with him. I didn't know my boyfriend and went somewhere with him. I didn't know anything. I was just a little naïve girl. I should have stayed at home and let my momma tell me what to do. I should have said no. I should have fought harder. I just want my bedroom, my basketball, my sisters, my brothers, my friends. God help me.

"Trust me I got her. I will take her home." And just like that I was back in his care. But he didn't care. He didn't protect me. I felt safer at that moment with him than I did with anyone else. He was all I knew. He just took my sex, hurt me, bruised my body, wanted sex all the time from me, just like the moment I met him when he put his hands in my pants. I just wanted him to get me home. I couldn't stop crying. The rain was coming down. I was wet. My clothes were wet. My pants were ripped. Damn, I like these pants. Even though they were hand-me-downs they were mine and now they are ripped down my thigh. My pants were ripped but my skin was untouched.

We walked a little bit more in silence before he said anything more. My cry slowed down to whimpers. I could hear him breathing. Then he said, "I am so sorry. He had that gun and he told me he would kill me if I didn't get out of the car and let him take you. He was going to rape you. He would have hurt you. I am so glad you jumped out of the car and you are ok." He was holding on to me tight. I didn't say a word. I was hurting. Rape me? Hurt me? This shit sounds so familiar. Except his uncle wasn't my boyfriend. My gut tells me he would have hurt me really bad. My gut tells me he may have used that gun on me. Is that what they do, take sex when someone doesn't want to give it to them?

"I want to go home. Please take me home," I said still whimpering. The tears would not stop. I was a runaway girl with no one looking for me and no one to truly love me.

"Come on. My friend from the other night will take us there." Another stranger. But this time I had a feeling I would be safe. The friend did what my boyfriend said the other night. "Let's go to my house real quick so you can change clothes. Your hair is curly now. Still pretty though." I wasn't flattered at all by his compliments. I didn't care about how my hair looked. All I cared about was being somewhere familiar and safe.

We went back to his house. He snuck me up to his sister room. She went off on him for letting something bad happen to me. My pants were ripped down the side of my leg from being caught on the car when I jumped. His sister gave me a towel to dry off and some more clothes to change into and told him he was buying her some more clothes to replace what she was giving me. He told her about their uncle and what happened. She eased off the insults. He left the room. After she helped me clean myself up he came back in to be with me. I sat there on the edge of the bed in someone else's clothes and I cried. After a few moments his sister came back into the room and told us to come on, so they could sneak me back out of the house.

We walked to his friend's house. I didn't want to go inside so he waited outside with me until his friend came to the door. I was thankful he had no problems taking me home. He felt sorry for me. He kept asking me if I was ok or needed anything. My boyfriend rode in the back seat with me. He was holding me and kissing me on my face and in my hair. At that moment I almost felt like he gave a damn about me.

Almost!

We pulled up in front of the building where Mary stayed. Police were there. "Ava, I can't get out, police are here, and I am not clean." I nodded. He kissed my forehead and my lips and gave me a hug. "Call me later ok." I started to walk away from the car and heard him say, "I love you Ava." Love me? Is this what love is? I kept walking. I knew he couldn't possibly love me.

I couldn't go home because I ran away. Mary's house was the only place I knew to go. I saw police and people everywhere, but I still walked up the stairs to Mary's house right into the middle of more madness.

Chapter 11
Home away from home

Everyone was shocked to see me walk up the stairs where the police were. They were looking for me. I knew they were. I didn't care. I didn't care about anything. When my mom saw me, she unleashed her demon and added to my hurt, added to my 'I don't give a damn' attitude. "You bitch, out here in these streets hoeing around. Come here you little Whore. I am going to beat your ass." She was screaming coming towards me.

"Ma'am calm down. Do you want me to take you to jail?" The police officer said to my mom.

"I know she been out here hoeing around. That's my daughter I can handle her how I want to handle her." My mom was irate.

"You called us. And right now you are not acting like a mother. I need to talk to your daughter and then I will come back to talk to you, but you need to be quiet," he said to her. He stood up to her. Wow was all I could say to myself. Another officer walked over towards her and he made everyone go down stairs.

The police officer that told my mom to shut up started talking to me after everyone went down stairs. "Are you Ava?"

"Yes sir," I said with my head held down and tears running down my face yet again.

"Did you run away from home?" He asked me in a soft voice. Somehow it felt like through his words he had compassion for me.

"Yes sir I did," I said. "Me and my mom got into a big fight. She always trying to hit me for no reason and she don't even know what be happening or if anything is wrong, she doesn't know how to be a mother and give love, or simply just listen," I said raising my voice a little out of frustration of my day, out of frustration from the escapade of having a boyfriend.

My mom heard me I guess. She was standing right below me. "I'm gon hit your ass alright. I am gon beat the whore out of you. Keep talking." I heard her yell up at me. I could hear some kids laughing. I could hear some people saying that's just wrong. I heard the officer tell her to come with him to get her away from hearing what me and the officer were saying.

"I can imagine how it was at home seeing how she is acting here. I'm assuming she has hit you before, do you want to press charges against her for hitting you?" I am not pressing charges against my momma, is he crazy? Who does that?

"No sir, I don't." I was looking down at my feet thinking about what my boyfriend's uncle did to me. That's who I want to press charges against.

"Are you ok Ava?" He asked me. He could tell I was hurting and deep in thought about something.

"No sir I am not. Bad things keep happening to me." Was all I could say.

"Bad things like what?" I was quiet. "I can help you Ava but only if you allow me to." Still I was quiet. I didn't know what to tell this man. What was I gonna say, my titties are too big, everybody wants to touch them. Men want to fuck me because of how I look, and I can't fight them because I am just a kid, I am not strong. No thank you. I didn't know how or even think he would believe me. "Well I don't think it would be wise for you to go home with your mom right now. But I am going to have to take you to juvenile. It will be people there for you to talk to if you decide you want to talk to anyone."

He pulled out handcuffs and was about to cuff me. "Can I please just walk with you and not be handcuffed sir. I promise I won't run." I wasn't no criminal. I didn't want to give anyone the satisfaction of seeing me in handcuffs.

"Not a problem. You seem like a good kid. Please don't run from me ok," he said trusting me but warning me at the same time.

"I promise. Thank you sir." And off to juvenile I was going. I walked down the stairs and pass the mob of people with my head up looking straight ahead. I could hear my siblings saying I love you sis. I would glance and give a half smile. I could also hear my mom still going off. Looking her in her eyes gave me chills to think that she hated me that much, at least that is what her actions screamed to me..

"Y'all better be taking her to jail. If I catch her in these streets again y'all will be taking me to jail." And this was my mother talking about me. Not an enemy. Not a stranger. My mother. How much more could I take of this life. Would it be better off without me? Would my mom be better off without me in her life? What did I do that was this bad to make her hate me? She doesn't even know what I have been through.

Maybe all of this was my fault. I shouldn't have let a boy touch my private parts. I shouldn't have let a boy trick me into thinking I was going shopping to get some new clothes which I never had. I shouldn't have gone inside the house to keep the dogs from eating me. I shouldn't have run away. I shouldn't have been somewhere where I knew no one and no one cared about me. I shouldn't have gotten in his uncle's car. Maybe everything is my fault. Maybe this is my punishment. I got into the back of the police car. I could see my sister crying. I loved my sibling's, but I didn't want to be around my mother. I couldn't understand. If I was surrounded by people who wanted to hurt me I might as well not be there. Go someplace where someone who was paid to protect me possibly would.

I was in juvenile for a few days. My mom came to see me, well she came to see the people who were holding me. She was talking calm. I was surrounded by hardcore girls who were in trouble for real stuff like robbing, stabbing, fighting, stealing cars and some more crazy bizarre stuff. They filled my head with all kinds of fuck your parent ideas. I had already had an I don't care anymore attitude so when they asked me if I was ready to go home I told them no. I told them I didn't want to go home with her that she didn't love me. Off to group home I went.

This place was like a big house. They fed me, I had to do chores, they played games and had all kinds of fun stuff going on here. Everyone could talk on the phone except for me. My mom told them I was not allowed so I wouldn't call my boyfriend. I didn't want to call him anyways. Some of the kids had visits from their family. I heard some of the kids say they wish they had family to come visit. After about a week my mom and siblings came to visit me. It was cool at first until my momma started asking me where I was that night. When I didn't want to answer her, she reverted back to her screaming. She had to leave. I was crying and upset, and I wasn't ready to go home.

Some girls were planning to sneak off and be with their boyfriends. They tried to get me to go but reality was, I was ok being there. I had good food. I wasn't ever hungry. I had clean clothes. Organized schedule, and I was surrounded by people who cared for me or at least pretended while they were working. It was easy to leave but I didn't want to. I felt safe for the first time in a very long time.

Because I didn't want to go back home, they sent me to a foster home where they send bad kids who needed discipline. Man were they hardcore.

When they moved me into the home they were ready for me. I had to stay in a room with five other girls and sleep in a bunk bed. It was like a crowded home but organized. There was a place for everything and they expected you to keep it all clean. These people would whoop their kids and foster kids with a belt if they didn't follow the rules and disobeyed. It was a real family bonded by something other than blood. Love.

Speaking of blood, they made me use tampons instead of pads. Said they had boys in the house and they didn't need to see that nasty blood. I wasn't trying to put anything inside me and still had trauma from being forced to have sex. It took me about ten minutes to figure out how to put a tampon in. Another girl in the house tried to teach me by showing me how quick and easy she slid one inside herself. That didn't help me out one bit. I thought maybe she is just open more. Funny now that I really think about that moment. Was she showing me she wasn't afraid to put something inside her sex spot? Not sure if it was a bragging moment or what but I was not a pro. I didn't use the tampons. I just used tissue instead since they wouldn't buy me any pads. I was surviving the best way I knew how.

They moved me to the room where the boys were for some reason and gave another girl my bed. I didn't care where I slept, I just did what they told me to do. I was in bed one night and the lady's son came in there talking to me. He reached up and touched my face. He told me how beautiful I was. He asked me if I ever had sex before. I kept telling him I don't know. He said the other girls let him touch them. I didn't know if I was supposed to or not. If I protested what would happen? I was sleeping in the same room. I shared a room with him and he could touch me whenever he wanted to while I was asleep. He told me he could make me feel good. He started touching the sides of my titties said he wanted to kiss me and he did on my chest and neck. He started sucking on one of my nipples. It did feel good. I didn't know how to tell him to stop. I don't know why it was so hard for e to say stop when I know something shouldn't be happening to me. Maybe it was the boy in the foster home telling me don't say anything or else. I got a beating after I spoke up. Or maybe it was the fact that I was raped and me pleading for him to stop got me hurt. I can't explain why I couldn't say stop other than I didn't know how, I was scared to.

One of the other girls saw him and told him she was telling his parents. He ran out after her. Then she blamed me said I was letting him touch me. I had to move out of that room and had to share a bed with a grown woman and a child. I wondered if that's why the other girl had to move out of that room. It was cool I guess. I felt safe in there. Moving me out of his room didn't stop him from touching me. He came in the bathroom with me one day and cornered me. I guess he liked what he felt when he touched me and kissed me. He got spooked that day, heard voices and didn't stay in the bathroom. I never reacted to him and he stopped trying. Besides he had other girls in the house to choose from that probably enjoyed him touching them. I heard rumors but didn't know if any of it was true.

I tried to use the phone one day to call my boyfriend and got in trouble. They had a recorder to listen to every call made in their home. They told me not to use the phone anymore that they would know. They didn't want me calling any boy trying to run off.

I made friends with the girl across the street. She let me use her phone sometimes. I called my boyfriend from her phone and talked to him once. I don't know why I even called him. I guess I wanted to feel love from someone even if it wasn't genuine love. He was the person I called my boyfriend, that took my sex from me, so at the moment he was the one to fill that void for me. He sounded funny, I could tell something was different. He did want me to run away with him. His voice scared me, and I didn't want to get in trouble. I wasn't planning to run anywhere with him.

A few days later I went to see my friend again and asked to see her phone. She told me she had to tell me something. She said her mom had to tell him to stop calling her house because he called one-night sounding like he was drunk or high or both wanting to speak to me, it was late. And I was surely not able to come out of the house or speak to him. Then he started talking nasty to her. He told her he wanted to eat her pussy out and fuck her hard. Her dad had to threaten him not to ever call his home again.

I started crying. I told her I was so sorry. I was embarrassed. I was hurt. And I was done with him hurting me. I no longer wanted to be his girlfriend nor wanted him to be my boyfriend. My mind was made up and I was done with him. I didn't feel like I could ever trust men saying they loved me. I didn't think any man would ever really love me. They would love my sex, love my body, love my beauty. But loving me was something I never felt and believed would be. My father didn't love me. He didn't even want me. Men sure as hell didn't love me. Real love does not hurt. If it did hurt, it shouldn't hurt long because that person who hurt you should know and fix it immediately.

I didn't know what real love was. Lust was not love. Kissing someone you didn't know wasn't love. Someone touching you that you barely know and didn't give permission to touch you wasn't love. Someone forcing you to have sex wasn't love.

What the hell was love?

I started school while I was in the foster home. I made a few friends and actually enjoyed being in this different atmosphere. But I was ready to go back home. I was done with my boyfriend. I didn't want to be a run a way. I wanted to be a good kid again. When I asked my foster mom when I was going back home she told me they wouldn't let me right now. I had to stay there for six months. Six months? I had been there for two months already, this was enough. I sobbed so hard on her bed snot was coming out of my nose. She told me I wasn't a bad kid and she didn't even see why I was there. She said she would tell them I was ready to go home and how good I had been. She said she would recommend it. I didn't get to go home until a month later. They made me stay for at least three months.

When I did go home I was super excited. I gained a lot of weight from eating so good every day. I guess being poor had its advantages to not over eat. There was a lot of over eating at the foster home. My friends were even excited to see me. They came to visit me and even talked about my weight gain, but it was cool. I knew they were genuinely my friends and saying it to my face was better than talking about me behind my back. They actually thought I was pregnant I had gained so much weight. After convincing them I wasn't, we talked until my mom wanted to call rank and have me come inside. I did what she said. I was excited to be home so whatever it took was what I was going to do.

I cleaned my momma house so spotless out of habit from the foster home. My old habits came back and things were getting back to normal. I was playing basketball again. The weight was dropping. And my relationship with my mom seemed better. Things were finally back to normal, so I thought.

Chapter 12
Normal as Normal could be

Life as I knew it was normal. I was back at school with my friends. I was back to playing basketball. I was back to listening to music in my room. I was back to being alone writing poetry. My mind was always in imagination mode. I made up stories and lived in a fantasy world inside my mind, wishing I had a different life mostly. My relationship with my mom was better. It was almost as if nothing bad ever happened. She was zoned out a lot, staying up all night and sleeping all day.

We had to wake ourselves up for school. Being late was normal for me. But I tried to get up on time so that I can walk to school with my friends. I didn't tell anyone about anything that ever happened to me. But I did feel like I was a part of the in crowd that was having sex. I now knew what they were talking about when they said having sex for the first time hurt. I knew what they were talking about when they said if you had a boyfriend you had to give him sex if you said you loved him and he said he loved you, even if it wasn't true. I now knew what they were talking about when they said if you didn't give your boyfriend sex they would take it from you.

But what I didn't know is that I still knew nothing. Everything that I learned was wrong. Just because you experience something bad didn't mean that was the norm, that it was right to be happening.

I didn't know that what happened to me was rape.

I didn't know that what happened to me was molestation.

I didn't know that what I experienced was assault on a minor.

I didn't know that no meant no.

I didn't know that I should have told someone, even if I thought they wouldn't listen.

And at that point of my life, I still didn't know right from wrong when it came to a man and a woman. I knew that my daddy wasn't there. At times I craved attention from a man, but at the same time was afraid to have attention from a man. Fearing he would hurt me. I knew that my mom didn't know how to show me love and it too made me crave that love. I knew nothing about love but what I felt in my heart was love. I knew everything about hate, it was all around me. I knew nothing about sexual pleasure but knew everything about sexual pain.

In some ways I felt like a kid again. I didn't complain about much. I went to school made good grades. I didn't have a boyfriend and didn't want a boyfriend. I thought boys were cute and may had a crush on a few, but I wasn't trying to have a boyfriend no time soon.

I was at home early one Saturday hanging out just being a kid and my mom tells me this man we all knew well wanted me to clean his house for some money. He was a drug dealer, so I knew he had money. He worked up under the man we called our uncle, so he was cool with our family. He was cute too and had a lot of ladies wanting him. I would hear conversations that were had about him at some of the gatherings where the ladies would be drinking.

My mom was money hungry, but I was excited to make some money even though I knew she would some kind of way end up with some of it, or most of it. She sent me up to his house. I was ready to clean whatever he needed me to clean. I was hoping he paid me a lot of money since he made a lot of money selling drugs. I assumed as a kid he did anyways.

When I arrived, he opened the door to let me in. First thing I saw was the kitchen. There wasn't many dishes dirty in the sink but I would still wash the few that were there up for him. I told him why I was there, and he didn't seem surprised. He told me he was waiting on me. So I asked him what he wanted me to do and where should I start. He told me to follow him. He led me back to a bedroom where I assumed I would have to fold clothes or something.

He started telling me what he wanted me to clean up and then he stopped. He grabbed me. He wrapped his long arms around me and he started kissing me. "What are you doing, stop."

"Just let me kiss you. You don't have to clean up anything I will still pay you," he said in my ear with his hot breath.

"I want to go home," I said. Fear was all over me. Not again! He was definitely a grown man. He was over six foot five inches and he was stronger than the boyfriend who took my sex. He was stronger than the uncle who tried to take my sex.

"You can go home when I am done. You won't get in trouble." I won't get in trouble?

What did he mean I won't get in trouble? This man is strong. Very strong. I couldn't get away from him. "Stop, please stop. You are hurting my arm." He had my arms twisted behind my back as he held them both together with one of his giant hands. He started to unbutton my pants. There was nothing I could do to stop him. I tried to squeeze my legs together, but he had too much power over me.

"I'm not trying to hurt you. I just want to fuck your beautiful ass." He turned me to the bed making me fall backwards on the bed with my hands behind my back. He let my hands go and pulled my pants and panties off of me in one quick pull. I tried to rise up. He pushed me back down with his upper body. My legs were closed shut. His penis was huge. He tried to push it in between my legs without even opening my legs.

"Stop. I don't want to have sex." I was getting mad. Yes, he was cute. Yes, all the girls wanted him. But I was a kid. I didn't want to have sex with him. I didn't even want him to be my boyfriend. He had a woman. He lives with her. In this very house. Where is his woman? Why is she not here having sex with him? Why does he want to have sex with me? Does my momma know he wanted to have sex with me? Did she send me up here to have sex with him? Is that why he said I won't get in trouble? Why is he doing this to me?

"Stop fighting me Ava. I know you are having sex. It will feel good. I have to have your pretty ass. You prance around here flaunting all that ass and titties. Stop fighting me. You are making it harder on yourself." He wasn't going to stop. I could feel his penis on me. I could feel it trying to go inside me. He kept pushing. I kept tightening my legs trying to prevent him from pushing inside me.

I was just a kid. I felt like I was fighting a grown man with no win in sight. I started crying and kept fighting. I didn't want him to take my sex. If I told on him to my play uncle I knew he would hurt him really bad if not kill him. If I tell my momma what would she do? Would she blame me? Say it's my fault? God who is going to save me? "I don't want to be hurt again please stop." I cried out one last time.

At that moment I heard him grunt in frustration and stop. He stood up. His penis was sticking straight out. "Put your clothes on," he said. He wasn't angry. Was he tricking me? He seemed mad but not at me. "Hurry up and get your clothes on," he said again. I quickly grabbed my clothes and began to put them on. He grabbed his pants and put them on. He watched me put my clothes on. "Look, don't tell anyone about this ok. Keep this between me and you."

"Okay," I said just wanting to get out of there. I wasn't planning to say anything to anyone no how.

He reached in his pocket and took out some money. "Here, take this money."

"No thank you I just want to go home." He came closer to me and I jumped. He put the money in my pants pocket.

"Take the money and don't tell anyone about what happened here."

"Can I leave now? I want to go home." I asked or said to him. Not sure if I was telling him what I was wanting to do or asking him for permission to leave. He had power over me at that moment and I wasn't as scared anymore but he could change his mind at any moment and try to take my sex again.

"You can leave unless you want to really help me clean." Hell no! I don't want to help you clean. I thought to myself. I just wanted to get out of his house.

"I will leave." I turned to leave and head home. I was relieved to be out of his house and headed home. I wiped my face so no one could tell I was crying. I forgot he put money in my pocket. When I got back home I started hanging with the other kids. My mom looked at me but didn't say a word. She didn't ask me if I helped him clean up. She didn't ask me how much money he gave me. She didn't say anything. That wasn't like my momma to not be nosey and not try to get money from me. She was like a vampire sucking blood. She wanted every dime she could get.

Something wasn't right about the situation. As a kid I didn't know any better. As a kid I was taught to trust my mom and at that moment I didn't know what happened. I trusted the wrong people and learned hard lessons along the way. This too was a learning lesson. I started to harden my heart against boys and men. I didn't trust them. Men in the neighborhood or not. Men that my mom dated or not. I didn't want a boyfriend and I didn't want to be around men again where they could hurt me.

I pretended like the incident never happened and I went back to being normal. I thought about telling, but since he wasn't able to put his penis inside me I felt like I won that battle on my own. I didn't say anything, and I didn't think about boys or men again. I pushed all the hurt and memories in the back of my mind. I didn't have any thoughts of being in another relationship no time soon that was until I met the boy on the balcony.

Chapter 13

His singing on the balcony

After about a year when all seemed to be going well, there he was. My neighbor's younger brother was standing on the porch when I looked out my window. I heard someone trying to get my attention and when I looked over in his direction I was struck by the sight of a handsome young man looking back at me. I smiled. Was he talking to me? Who was he? I have never seen him here before. I only saw my neighbor once. She just moved in not too long ago. I pulled my head back inside the window quickly. Blushing. Scared to go back outside. I didn't want him seeing me.

He waited until my brother was outside and asked about me. I stayed in my room. I didn't look out the window anymore. Then I heard someone throwing rocks at my window. I figured it was him.

"Ava." I heard him calling my name. My brother had to have told him my name.

I walked over to the window to look out. "How do you know my name?" I looked over to where he was standing and asked.

"Your brother told me your name," he said. "I don't bite, I promise. Come outside." I was not going outside.

"I am busy right now," I said and closed my window.

"Ok I will be waiting on you all day and all night if I have to," he said loud enough for me to hear.

I stuck my head back out the window. "You are loud." What did I say that for?

"I am going to keep being loud until you come outside and talk to me pretty lady. Oooh Ava, oooh Ava." He started singing. He sounded awful, like dogs would start howling at any moment awful. But I was smiling because of his song. It was awful, but cute.

It was cute. It was sweet. But I wasn't going outside. My sister and my brother came in the house telling me some boy wanted me outside. I simply said, "I know," and stayed in my room. I was not ready to talk to him. He wanted me to come outside so bad that he tried to get anyone he could to come tell me. I was fourteen now, but I still didn't think I wanted another boyfriend. I was happy just being me all by myself. I didn't go outside at all that night. I stayed in my room listening to music and writing poetry.

He wanted to get my attention

He saw me before I saw him

It was like Adam to Eve

It was like a cool summer breeze

Grazing my beauty with a gush of wind

His eyes were watching me

Turning to see who I am

Demanding my attention

I too glanced my eyes upon a sight to see

I panicked and didn't want his eyes

Upon my face seeing me

I smiled too at the pleasant sight

He wanted to know who the girl was

Hiding behind the walls
My name he repeatedly called
Rocks at my windows and then
His singing on the balcony
Desperate is he…

I stopped writing at the sound of more rocks gently hitting my window. They must have been small pebble rocks because they were soft pecks loud enough for me to notice but quiet enough that no one else in the house could hear. I was surprised to hear the rocks and even more so to see that he was standing outside my window. I opened the window and decided to talk to him, see what he wanted. "What?" I said trying not to but blushing at the sight of him.

"You didn't come outside all day. I was waiting on you." How did he know I didn't come out all day? Is he stalking me?

"How do you know I didn't come out at all? You stalking me?"

"I guess I am. I didn't want to miss you. You are so pretty. I would wait forever just to talk to you." That was sweet. I was really blushing. "Nothing wrong with talking is there pretty little lady?" He was really trying to win me over. He was quite the charmer.

I was smiling. I was falling weak to his words and I gave in. "Ok, I can come out tomorrow, it's kind of late tonight."

"Well can you stay in the window and talk to me? Just for a little while." He didn't want me to leave. He wanted to keep me there. I was thinking on what I should do and if I even wanted to continue talking. "I am not ready for you to leave me. I waited all day to see you. Pretty please." He said with his lips poked out trying to portray he would be sad if I said no.

"Well, I am still here so I guess that's a yes," I said with an attitude and a smile.

"You a little feisty huh. Pretty and feisty." Feisty was something new for someone to call me but I was giving him a challenge. More so because I had my guards up around my heart to prevent anyone from hurting me.

"I don't know anything about you. I don't know your name, age or where you stay." I didn't really know what else to ask.

"My name is Romeo. I am sixteen years old. I stay with my mom mostly, she lives in Atlanta, but my father lives here. My sister just moved in upstairs and I came down to help her. My dad stays ten minutes away and I might be staying here during the summer." He was giving me a lot of information all at once.

"You sixteen. I'm only fourteen. And Atlanta is far from here." I tried to comment on some of his information he stated about himself.

"Age is just a number. You look older than fourteen. You are not telling me the wrong age are you?" Why does everyone think I am lying about my age?

"I am really fourteen. I just look older I guess." My body was older than fourteen, but I was only fourteen.

"I don't care how old you are, you are still pretty." He was giving me compliments and making me smile every time.

"Thank you," was all I could say. I guess I was going to be nice to him. He was nice to me. And he was cute.

I stayed in the window talking to him for over an hour. It got really cold outside. He put his hands in his pockets to warm them. After too long it was unbearably cold, and he decided to go inside. I promised him I would come out the next morning when I got up. And to my surprise he was up early in the morning. I could hear him throwing more rocks at my window.

"Ava." I heard a voice calling in a loud whisper. I never had anyone pursue me as he was. I lived right next door to where he was staying and even that was not close enough for him. I rolled over and went back to sleep. It was too early on a Saturday to be up.

A few hours later I woke up, took a bath and made myself pretty. I washed my hair and wore it down curly. I wanted to be sure he was still interested in me. I said I didn't care about boys but there was something different about him. He seemed to be interested in me and not just my body.

I went outside on my front porch and what do you know he was sitting outside on the balcony of his sister's front porch.

I pretended not to see him turning my back to him because I was blushing. "Sleeping beauty has awakened." That did it. I was smiling big time now. I couldn't believe he was sitting outside waiting on me.

I turned to look at him unable to control my smile. "Hey." I couldn't think of anything else to say.

He was standing up close to the rail of the balcony with a book in his hand. "I can't believe you are actually outside. My heart is beating fast. You make me nervous." He made me laugh he was acting so dramatic.

"What are you reading?" I asked him. I didn't like reading at the time and didn't really care what he was reading, I was just making conversation.

"It's a book we have to read over the summer for school. It's actually pretty good. Helped me to pass some time by until you woke up."

"Oh, ok are you a nerd or something?" Only nerds would read books when they didn't have to right? I had never met anyone who would read a book and didn't have to read.

"Not a nerd," he said and laughed. "I just love to read books. Stay right there I'm coming down," he said and in a flash he was standing by my porch close to me.

"That was fast," I said. I sat down on the side of the porch with my legs hanging. He stood to the side of me. I was a bit nervous too. I didn't know what to do or say. This was all new for me.

"Wow. You look even prettier up close." He was blushing.

"You keep saying that," I said. That's all he kept saying was how pretty I was.

"Well it's true. You are the prettiest girl I have ever seen," he said looking me in my eyes.

"Thank you. That's the nicest thing anyone has ever said to me." I think I like this boy.

"So, what do you like to do?" he asked.

"I like to write and listen to music mostly. I like basketball too."

"Oh yeah? You like to write but not read?"

"Reading, not really unless it's something I wrote. Writing is more interesting. I can create my own stories." We were having a normal conversation.

"You would be surprised what you could read inside a book." He leaned on the porch turning his body towards me. He reached up and touched my hair. "Your hair is so pretty." I smiled.

At that moment his sister was on the porch looking down at us. "Romeo, can you go to the store for me please? I need some milk." She was pretty. She didn't seem too friendly though.

"Ok," he answered his sister. "Can you walk to the store with me?" he turned and asked me.

"Sure, I will walk with you."

"Let me go get some money. I will be right back."

I waited for about five minutes until he walked back down the stairs. I can't believe I actually waited that long for anyone and didn't leave. I thought, I must really feel some kind of way for him to actually wait and not disappear.

We walked to the store together talking every step of the way. He even bought me something to drink. Back then that was considered a real special treat. No one had money to buy anything but the necessities those days. We mostly had to drink water at home. If we had Kool-Aid and sugar, we were living the life.

Romeo was the perfect gentleman with me. I appreciated him for that. I waited for him outside his sister's place on the second floor and stayed there for a while talking with him. I was starting to enjoy his company and his conversation when he dropped the words I wasn't expecting to hear.

"I leave to go back home to Atlanta tomorrow." Why would he be trying to talk to me if he knew he wouldn't be here to see me? I would not be able to call him because it was long distance and it would cost too much money. So what does this all mean?

"Oh, I see. So, I won't see you anymore?" Those were my initial thoughts! Why would he work so hard to get me to talk to him and act like he like me just to be leaving?

"I will be back to visit during school breaks, some during the summer, and holidays. My dad comes down to Atlanta sometimes and I even thought about moving here. I will come back to visit a lot." Ok so he will come to visit what does that mean for me?

"That's cool. Maybe I will see you when you come back. I mean you will have other people to visit." What makes me special to think he will only come back to see me.

"Well I was hoping to see you every time I come back to visit." Oh ok.

"Why do you want to see me every time you come back?" I didn't really know what he wanted from me. Surely he didn't want to be just my friend. He was making me feel all warm inside and I kind of liked it. I was really hoping he didn't want us to be just friends.

"I like you. I mean, I really like you. You are a beautiful girl. I want you to be my girlfriend." Did he just ask me to be his girlfriend? I was quiet looking at him. "Will you be my girlfriend Ava?" Ok now he was asking.

"Yes," I said with a smile. He then picked me up and swung me around. Still holding me in the air he did something I wasn't expecting. He kissed me in the mouth and his tongue pierced my lips. I had never been kissed like this before, it was more than a simple kiss. At first, I didn't know what to do, and then I followed his lead kissing him back as he was kissing me. Our tongues danced as our lips were pressed together. His hands were wrapped around my body so tight. They were around my back and they stayed there as he gently placed me to my feet.

He didn't touch me inappropriately. I felt safe. I felt cared for. I felt respected. I felt something I never felt before. My stomach felt funny, I had butterflies. It wasn't like my ex-boyfriend forcefully taking my sex, or his uncle or my mom's friend. It was completely different, and it made me feel different. He kissed me for about five minutes.

"Wow that was amazing. You are a great kisser."

"Thanks," I said smiling.

"I have wanted to do that ever since I saw you yesterday." He was making me blush. He was blushing harder than I was. He was acting like a little happy kid.

"So, what do we do now? I mean you are leaving tomorrow and really we just met. What do we have to hold on to?"

"We can hold on to the feelings we are sharing and knowing that I will be back. We can write letters back and forth and I will be back before you know it."

And just like that I had a new boyfriend. But this time I felt good about having a boyfriend. There was no disrespect. There was no violation of him touching me when I didn't want to be touched and he didn't try to take my sex. He didn't try to lure me into a space to be alone with him behind closed doors. He even stood outside in the cold breezy night just to talk to me. I think I like my new boyfriend!

He gave me an entire new thought process on having a boyfriend and in a way, he was teaching me what having a boyfriend should really be like. He was teaching me something different than the girls in the bathroom at school talking about sex. He was teaching me something different than what my mom never taught, nor my dad.

This was a good teaching, one that would redirect all the old thoughts of what I thought was supposed to happen with boys, but instead what should happen, and what should not happen. I was embracing this new experience. I was embracing this new outlook hoping that all the bad I experienced would disappear deep in my memory to be replaced by something pleasant and desired.

Chapter 14
Let's Take a Moment

Being a young female, there are so many fears of what if's. Young girls face life changes with their bodies, hormones, making friends, and let's not forget about boys just to name a few. Not knowing what if's can be so scary for anyone but especially a young girl growing up from childhood to teen-hood. These years can be some of the toughest times. But what a young girl needs most to cope and overcome the difficult times is the love from her parents.

A kind ear and an open mind.

To feel love.

To know that she matters and its ok to be uniquely her.

To know that she has someone in her corner looking out for her that she can go to for anything that she needs, even if it's just to talk, vent, cry, or simply be held in her parents loving arms with no judgement.

Some people have both parents at home, some may have only one, or someone other than their parents like a grandparent or aunt. Just because you are there living in the home doesn't mean that all is well. Doesn't mean that you "are there." Stop for a moment to ask your children, "are you ok? Do you need anything?" Give them a hug that last more than a quick second.

As a child I craved love, and even though my mom was at home, she was there in the same house, she didn't know how nor did she show me love, at least not in the way I desired with words, affection, and teaching me life's lessons, even if she didn't know all the answers. I didn't see love and I didn't feel love.

I searched for that love within myself because I refused to just allow anyone to love me. But that lack of love made it easier for someone to come along and pretend to love me, to use me for their selfish reasons to get what they wanted from me.

I didn't have anyone to teach me, to prepare me, to protect me.

Life experiences taught me.

Even if the teachings were wrong.

Parents are supposed to take care of their children and protect them from the predators of the world. Protect them with wisdom to know what to do in bad situations and how to try and avoid bad situations. Protect them from seeking love because of a lack of it at home. Parents are supposed to protect their children in every aspect of caring for and teaching them.

It only takes a moment to say I love you.

A few minutes of your twenty-four-hour day to stop and have a conversation with your child, make sure they are ok emotionally, physically, socially and even psychologically.

Let them know you care.

Hugs are free and priceless when given. Hugs are easy. Are remembered. Are needed. They are the starters for conversations of a caring heart. The gateway to open up the start of a conversation.

Parents, make sure your child knows and feel your love for them so that they never have to seek love because they lack love. Not all love they find is good for them and you never want them to confuse genuine love with negative behavior that pretends to love for the sake of manipulating just to use and abuse. Show your children love for the sake of protection. Show them love so that when life's moments of heartache, hurt, pain, confusion come, they will come back to that love. They will come back to you for help, for guidance, for that hug, for comfort.

Rape, molestation, assault on a minor, none of that should ever be accepted as being ok ever. Never! Never! Never! Never! And I mean NEVER is it ok for anyone to harm you sexually, violate your private areas, or in any kind of way.

No always mean no.

Stop always means stop.

No one has the right to take from you what you don't want to give. Never!

Parents have that conversation with your children!

And yes, it is okay to tell someone. You don't have to hold any pain inside because of fear. You don't have to be ashamed or embarrassed. Someone will listen. Keep telling until someone hears you loud and clear. It's never too late to speak up and release the pain held inside. Love yourself more, love yourself and know that you are enough, you are precious, you are beautiful, and your beauty should never be a curse.

Parents pay attention and love your child even when you think they don't need you. Take it from someone who did need a mother who wasn't "there" but visibly there. It doesn't take much. You gave birth to a blessing that God saw fit to give to you. Take care of that blessing. Love that blessing. It's not too late to start today. Keep trying because your efforts are noticed and do make a difference.

Love should never hurt but should be felt through words, kindness and wanted affection. Parents start loving your children now in many ways, through what you say, how you say it and simple acts of love like a simple hug or simply saying the words and why you love them.

Be there and show up!

Yes, it does matter!

Mom, it does matter!

Dad, it does matter!

Chapter 15
Long Distance

This long-distance relationship was new for me and different. When he left, I wished he could stay a while longer but anticipated the day he would return. Until then I would hold on to the memory of the day we met. I didn't really know if he was coming back. I didn't know what to expect. But what he showed me was respect and kindness. I felt his genuineness. I felt that he really liked me. I didn't think he wanted anything from me except to be in my presence, in my space, and for me to be in his. That was an amazing feeling. Even if I never saw him again I would hold on to that memory.

The day he left I was sad, but I didn't understand why seeing as how I had just met him the day before. It didn't seem as if we had just met. We talked from the time I came outside that day until it was time for him to leave. We talked about everything. He made me laugh, made me smile, and I felt good inside being with him. He was such a gentleman. He didn't try to touch me inappropriately and when he wanted to kiss me he asked if it was ok.

The way he kissed me was like magic. It felt right. I was falling for this boy even though I wanted to ignore him when he was trying to get my intention. He treated me how I would want a boyfriend to treat me. Complete opposite of what I experienced before him. He made me reconsider having a boyfriend and rethink what the girls said in the school bathroom to be true.

You don't have to have sex when you have a boyfriend, some boys just like you and want to be in your space. Having a boyfriend doesn't have to be painful, doesn't have to be stressful, or fearful.

When he was leaving that day, I released a tear. You would have thought we were together for months the way we were acting. He hugged me for what seemed like forever, picking me up off my feet spinning me around. His dad teased him a bit. I became friends with his sister because her little brother liked me so much. And when it was time to leave, all the excitement of having him there quickly left and I was consumed with sadness. It was ok if he didn't come back because I now knew what a comfortable relationship felt like. I now had something better to base what a relationship could possibly feel like and be like. My two-day experience was more of a "feel good, right way" teaching than my entire life before that moment.

A couple days went by and I had already continued my normal routine. But I lit up when I realized I had a letter in the mailbox from him. My smile was endless. My heart was beating with anticipation. My stomach was in knots. I ripped it open on my way to my room closing the door behind me so I could read the letter in private.

Hello beautiful, I wanted to send you a letter as soon as I got home so you would know I was thinking about you. The entire ride back I talked about you to my dad. He thinks you're great. I wish I had a picture of you but I have you etched in my memory. I am so glad you came out to talk to me and said yes to being my girlfriend. You are so beautiful. I saw you out the window from my sister's apartment and I was glued to the window until you went into your home. That day I made it my only mission to get to know who the girl behind the beauty was. Ava, beautiful Ava, girlfriend. I can't wait to see you again…

His letter was six pages long full of sweet words about me. He also told me more about who he was. We exchanged letters back and forth for a couple months. He sent me pictures and I sent him pictures. He even sent me a tape full of songs he added himself that made him think about me. I listened to the tape every day and all day. I read his letters over and over hoping that he did the same. Writing letters was exciting to me because I loved to write. I wrote poems just for him and added them in with the letters I wrote back. He was so sweet to even send me stamps through the mail to make sure I could send him letters back.

He would visit his dad or his sister often surprising me when he came. I loved his surprises. We would spend as much time as possible together when he came. He was truly my boyfriend and made me feel so special, so pretty, so wanted, so like a girlfriend.

The first summer after we met was both exciting and sad. My mom actually allowed me to see him and spend time with him. She had the hots for his dad. Me and Romeo spent so much time together from the time we woke up until it was time to go to sleep.

I was crazy about him.

I loved being with him.

I loved the letters we would write.

I loved the way he made me feel.

I loved him.

Every time he would leave I became sad. He was a part of my life, a good part of my life. A part of my life that I looked forward too. I became dependent on him to make me feel good, to make my heart feel full. I was still learning to love me and when he came into my life, I stopped learning.

I started loving him. I didn't even know what I wanted out of life, but I knew in my mind that I loved him. I didn't know what it meant to be in love or what it meant to have a boyfriend. I didn't know if I was a good girlfriend or not. I didn't know if I was supposed to feel the way I felt or if what I felt was even love. But at that moment in my life, he was just what I needed to survive.

After the back and forth with all the love letters and sporadic visits from him, our relationship was at a high point then calmed down a bit. We dated for about two years before it died off. The long distance took its toll on us and we eventually grew apart. It was hard at first knowing that what we shared was diminishing and we both were moving on with our lives. Once it started happening I remember being sad, but I valued everything he taught me about love and what it meant to be in a functional two-sided relationship. He was truly my prince charming. He was the first boy I ever loved.

I started learning more and more about myself. I learned how to avoid hurtful harmful situations with men. To not put myself in situations where I could possibly become over powered and victimized when my no's would be unheard. All was looking good in my life and I was about to turn sixteen years old. This was an exciting age for me. I was single. I was starting to embrace my beauty. I was getting older and soon would become an adult. I felt wiser. I felt stronger. I had experienced hurt and pain in my life and I had also experienced love. I had two more years and I would become an adult. I was ready, so I thought.

Chapter 16
Sixteenth birthday

I was finally sixteen and my mom had just received a settlement check she had been waiting on, so she decided to throw me a party. It wasn't anything too fancy, but it was my party. She had food and a cake. She got one of the guys from the neighborhood to bring his big ass speakers and be the DJ for the night. The music was loud, and people started to come from everywhere to party with me.

I was happy so many people were there at my house party. Everyone was dancing, eating and having a great time. About an hour into the party someone bumped the DJ table and the music stopped. It is so funny when I think about that situation now. Someone screamed out "ah man the DJ sucks, I'm out of here," and that was enough for the majority of the crowd to bounce. They left my party. The only people that was left were my real friends and my siblings. I didn't care. I was excited about the time I did have a large crowd at my party, but I enjoyed the smaller intimate setting more with people who I knew were my family and friends.

The most exciting part of that night was receiving a gift from my mom. I don't recall anything else in my life that my mom has ever bought for me, but on this night, she gave me a beautiful white gold ring. I never had a good relationship with my mom so that ring meant a lot to me.

Since the party was basically over the grown folks turned it into a grownup party drinking and smoking. My brother had got his hands on some weed and told me since it was my birthday I had to take a puff. I tried and choked. I couldn't stop coughing. He decided I couldn't smoke but instead blew me a "shotgun." He blew the smoke into my mouth and I had to inhale. I still choked but I was high.

My mom and her friends were drunk, and she decided since it was my birthday she would give me a beer. I had never drank beer before but I was trying to be cool for my birthday and drink with the grown-ups. That stuff was so nasty. The more I drunk of it, the more I started to accept the taste. I was drunk. No one was paying attention to me besides the bi-sexual lady and her boyfriend, my mom's neighborhood friends. When the bi-sexual chick passed out drunk her boyfriend invited me into his apartment to show me something. No one cared where I was even though I was drunk. They were drunk, more so than me.

This man was well into his thirties. He told me he wanted to give me a birthday gift and started to kiss me. I couldn't even stand up without someone helping me I was so messed up. He ended up undressing me even though I told him no. That grown ass man had his way with me that night. He was so rough. He was having sex with me so hard and so fast. I remember hanging off the bed and he didn't stop to pull me back up. He was so focused on having hard fast sex with me that my entire small framed body was jerking so hard I started to throw up. He didn't stop until he had an orgasm. Me throwing up should have been enough to make him stop but he didn't. Me saying no should have made him stop but it didn't.

I felt so disgusted.

I was sixteen and drunk.

I should have had someone watching me.

I shouldn't have been allowed to drink.

I shouldn't have been left alone.

Left alone with a grown ass man who took advantage of a sixteen-year-old drunk girl.

Momma!

Daddy!

Romeo!

Somebody!

No one came to save me. When he was done with me, he sent me out the door telling me not to say anything to anyone. I stumbled home. I fell on the front porch scraping my knees. I kept throwing up. My head was spinning. I was so drunk. I was so sick. I was so hung over. I felt bad. I felt so all alone.

I looked down at my hand and remembered my momma gave me a ring for my birthday. I smiled for a moment through all the pain I was feeling. I knew at that moment that this too was another hard life lesson I had to learn.

I'm never drinking again, I said screaming to myself out loud.

My birthday was a day to remember, a day I would never forget. So much was going on and so much happened. I went from having a good time to some perverted old ass man preying on me. He knew exactly what he was doing, waiting, watching, and waiting. He waited for the right time to lure me away when no one was paying attention. When everyone should have been paying attention.

I felt so nasty afterwards. Disgusting. I wasn't even attracted to him. He was not even my boyfriend. He was a grown man. Someone that my mom was hanging out with. How could that happen to me on my birthday.

I thought I was wiser, but mixing alcohol with trying to enjoy yourself around people who really don't care about you was another bad idea.

My mom cared about me I am sure, after all I am her daughter. But she was in no state of mind to pay attention. She should have paid attention. I didn't want that nasty old man to take my sex. I couldn't stop him. Why do men think they can just take something from a woman just because they want to? Just because they see a pretty girl. I should have spoken up and told someone. I shouldn't have been drinking. I should have screamed.

Now I had another life lesson learned and something else I had to try and avoid. My mom's friends. Why me? I felt like I was a magnet for men to do whatever they wanted to me and I was afraid to speak up. I was afraid to say something to someone. Why didn't he have sex with his girlfriend who was right there drinking with him. Was she not good enough? She was a grown woman. Damit! Why me?

When I was in that foster home ten years earlier and the little boy that laid on me told me not to tell anyone or else… what did "or else" mean?

When his mom told me not to ever repeat or tell anyone what her son did to me, she beat the crap out of me afterwards for repeating it, pleading my case to make her believe me.

When I was raped by my so-called boyfriend and wanted to go home and tell my momma, I never got the chance to. She beat me black and blue before I could utter one word. That hurt deeper than the billions of bruises to my body. It hurt me deep in my heart, deep in my soul.

And what about the guy whose house my mom sent me to clean up, he tried to take my sex. My mom sent me to him and he told me not to tell anyone. What would have happened if I did?

If I would have told someone about any of those things, what would have happened? Fear had a hold on me.

Would the foster parents have tried to drown me in the tub or worse? Would my mom have never beat me, would she have listened, called the police, go to his house and confront him? Would my play uncle have killed the man who tried to rape me?

Would that old man who had his way with me on my sixteenth birthday have gone to jail?

I had to deal with what happened to me the best way I could. Bottle it up. Bury it in my mind. Escape through writing and music. I had no one to talk to, no one to save me, no one to teach me what to do. I had no one.

I should have been protected.

I should have been comfortable telling someone.

I didn't know. I didn't know how to tell anyone. I didn't know.

I was afraid.

I was afraid of the "Or else."

Chapter 17
Learning Love

I had to figure out what love really was and what it was not. I realized quickly that there were so many different types of love, or what was said to be love. I had to decipher what love really was, what love I wanted, and what "love" I never desired to have again. That pretend love tainted me. Scared me. Hurt me. I never wanted that type of love in my life ever again.

There were people all around me who said they loved me, but they never loved me, or at least I didn't see or feel their love. The word love was thrown around loosely where I grew up. It did not have any true meaning to go by. I don't even think people knew what it meant to be in love, to feel love, to give love, or receive love. If I had to guess, it was only used when someone wanted something from you or someone else. If someone really did love you their actions always supported the spoken or unspoken words.

But me, I had so much love in my heart to give. I wanted to love and be loved. I naturally craved love. The storyteller in me was always active, imagining fairytales happening in my life, imagining a different right now, imagining a different future, a different ending. I was always lost in my imagination of something more, something better. But I had to learn love, learn love's language from the standpoint of my neighborhood. I had to learn how to know when someone really loved me, or if they wanted something from me. I was a giver, still am, but I would naturally want to give.

I had to learn that I couldn't be nice to everyone, I couldn't engage in friendly conversation with just anybody, I couldn't hang out in certain places. I couldn't give anyone a reason to want to "say they love me" when really, they only desired something from me. My niceness was mistaken for an invitation to hurt me, touch me, have your way with me. My conversations were an invitation to break my heart, to tell me things that had no truth to it, to try to manipulate me with words that had no truth to them. Hanging out was just an invitation for the thirsty men, the perverts, the drunks, those that were high off whatever drug was popular, to try to take my sex or at least use me as a sex symbol to lust after with their hands, with their dirty words.

Even when I thought I knew, I didn't know everything. I was still learning the hard way. Through living life and experiencing things first hand. But as I learned, I tried not to ever make the same mistake twice. But I still craved to be loved. I would have taken the love from my mother, but she didn't know how to give love. I would have taken the love from my father, but he was not in my life.

I started to manipulate boys that I thought were cute, that I thought would not hurt me or try to take advantage of me. I talked to them more. I flirted. And I entertained them, enough for them to give me some affection. I even thought about "playing the field" and making several boys my boyfriend. But the scared little girl in me kept me from going too far, from starting something new that could ultimately hurt me. I have never known a man nor a boy who wanted to share a girl or their woman. That was a recipe for disaster for sure.

I was still learning. Even when I thought I knew I really didn't know. As a child, there is so much to soak up from the world, but it should never be taught by the world. Parents should teach their daughters about love, about what's right and what's wrong. Not the streets. Not from experiencing the wrong. Not from the girls at school in the bathroom. Not from being hurt so many times that she thinks it was how it was supposed to be until someone else shows them differently.

What was love really? I read what love was in the bible.

I knew love was never supposed to hurt.

I knew love included being patient, being kind.

I knew love was about the truth.

I knew love was not associated with wrong doing, evil, hurt, heartache.

But what was love in its entirety? How was I supposed to determine if what someone was proclaiming to me to be love was really love? I thought I knew but sometimes I was still fooled.

"Baby you know you the only girl for me." Okay sure, the words and actions don't align when some other girl is checking for them and they meet at a party and he dancing and grinding on her bootie.

"That girl don't mean nothing to me." I bet you tell all the girls that to make them feel special just to get in their panties.

"You are the most beautifuliest girl in the whole wide world. I am in love with you girl, love at first sight." Ok thank you. I have been told before. Just because you think I am beautiful doesn't mean you in love or that I am going to fall in love. You just making a statement.

I am trying to weed out the punk ass mother "fakers" who want something from me. If they don't just want something, I guess they will stick around, keep trying even through my sarcasm attitude. Everyone seemed to want a piece of the beauty they see, but there is so much more to me than the beauty that is on the outside. What about the beauty on the inside?

I wish I had my mother there to teach me the difference in what was love and what was not love. One thing I knew for sure was that it would take a lot for a man to just win my heart and love me. Falling in love is what young girls wanted to do. Falling in love was a desire, a dream for young girls. But I was different. Love had tainted me. Love almost destroyed me. If I didn't love myself and desire that same love in return I would have given up on love. But I didn't.

I wanted to be loved.

Genuinely loved. Truly loved.

Loved unconditionally.

I wanted love around me.

I wanted the same kind of love I wanted to give.

I was being choosey about love.

I weeded out the bad and never seeming true love.

I wanted love. I was learning love.

Chapter 18

Father Hear my cry

I would often wonder why my father was never around. Why he chose to not see me. I remember being a little girl riding in his black truck a few times. I was such a happy little girl during those rides with my daddy. But that was just a very few times. My dad would come by the house late at night to see my mother every now and then and sometimes they would wake me up to see him just before he would leave. I am sure he was only there to get "something" from my momma. Seeing me was more like an added task just because he was there. To me the visits didn't last long. I was only aware he was there right when it was time for him to leave.

I know now that I wasn't his reason for visiting. But as a kid those few moments made me smile. It was the time after he was gone that was sad. And the time in between what felt like an eternity seeing him again that was sad. With every short visit I would cry for him to stay. But the tears meant nothing. He never heard my cry. He would leave our home and I would cry myself to sleep.

I cried for him to stay.

I cried for him to see me.

I cried for him to be in my life.

I cried for his love.

I cried for his affection.

I cried for his attention.

I wanted my father in my life. I wanted him to love me, to be there for me, to let me love him. But he wasn't, and he didn't. Those popup visits gave me hope but it was full of broken promises and dreams of having a father in my life shattered. He didn't listen. He didn't want to hear me. He didn't want to be there for me.

Many nights I would sit up wondering what my daddy was doing. Wonder if he was thinking about me. I even found a number to call him and I remember asking to speak to my daddy. It was close to Christmas and I was so happy I had the right number. They asked me who my daddy was and I had to say his name before they went to get him. I was on hold for what seemed like forever. I know it had to be five minutes before he got on the phone.

"Hey daddy, what you doing?"

"Hey, who is this."

"This your daughter Ava, duh. I found your number to call you."

"Oh ok. Hold on a second."

"Ok, hurry up daddy I already been on hold for a long time."

A few more minutes passed as I waited on my daddy to come back to the phone. It sounded like they were having a party or something. I could hear a lot of people and music playing in the background. He finally came back to the phone. "Hello."

He said it as if he was surprised I was still there. "Hey daddy. What took you so long?"

"Oh, I'm sorry. What you doing?"

"I was making my Christmas list for you."

"Oh yeah, what you want for Christmas?"

"I want a lot of stuff. I want a bike, some clothes, some shoes, some fingernail polish…" I continued on telling him my Christmas list and what my sisters wanted. He put me on hold again. He didn't say anything else for a long time. I could still hear the party going on. I waited on the phone for over thirty minutes. Everyone kept telling me to hang up he wasn't coming back but I didn't want to hear that. I wanted to wait on my daddy because I knew he didn't forget about me. I was his daughter. I kept screaming his name through the phone hoping he would hear me. I started crying still screaming his name to come back to the phone. I wanted him to hear me. I was screaming. I was crying. He didn't hear me. He didn't hear my cry.

After screaming and crying for so long I heard someone picking up the phone and I was thinking my screams paid off, he finally heard me, but the phone went dead. Someone hung up on me…

My siblings tried to console me. My heart was broken. All I wanted was for my father to hear my cry. I wanted my daddy to love me. I wanted him to see me. I cried myself to sleep that night. I never received any Christmas gifts I asked him for. I can't even remember when it was that I saw him again after that day. My thoughts of my daddy changed that night. I was heartbroken. I was disconnected from his love. I didn't know my daddy. I didn't have a father...

I was sixteen when I called my father again. I talked so direct to him, with so much anger in my voice. I resented him for not being in my life. His wife was ease dropping on our conversation. She was listening as I talked about his last visits and our last phone call. She could hear how angry and hurt I was. He finally told her to hang up the phone. I asked him if she was the reason why he didn't want to be in my life. He answered as if he was scared. As if he was ashamed. I cried my last cry that day. I reminded him of the pain he caused me. I wanted him to hear and feel my pain.

Why wasn't I enough for him to love? I needed my father. Didn't he know that I needed him? Daughters need fathers.

Father, hear my cry...

Looking back, my Heavenly Father was there comforting me, protecting me, guiding me on a journey that I needed to take in life to make me a better person, a better wife, a better mother. My journey without my father made my journey with my Heavenly Father stronger. Yes, bad stuff happened to me, but I learned life lessons and became a stronger little girl, wiser before my time, a stronger young lady with a desire to change generational curses. My father never heard my cry, but my Heavenly Father heard every cry. I became stronger in a life lived that should have broken me. I am not broken. My hard life did not consume me, did not destroy me, did not keep me bonded to my past.

Every daughter needs her Father.

Chapter 19
Rebel in the making

After my sixteenth birthday and the call with my father, I found myself wanting to be a rebel with everything in life. I was so angry about the things that were still happening to me and has happened to me throughout the years. It all came rushing back to me like a flood destroying the world. All of it was destroying my mind. What happened to me on my sixteenth birthday and the rejection of my father yet again made me angrier, and rage was over me. I was hurting. In my mind I wanted to hurt other people. I wanted my pain to go away so why not be a rebel, act out, do things to hurt other people. That seems to be the way of the world these days.

I tried to convince myself not to care about anything anymore, how other people felt, thought of me, how I even felt. I started to shut down my feelings. I wanted to stop being so sensitive, so worried about others, so kind hearted. In my mind I was a rebel in the making.

I hate them for what they did!

All of them!

I hate them for hurting me!

All of them!

I hate that my beauty is a curse!

I hate they think they can just touch me, rape me, take my sex away from me, disown me, disrespect me, lie to me!

Why me?

I can show them evil.

I can play their lack of love games.

Their pretend games.

I started manipulating the minds of little boys, young men, making them think they had a chance with me. In return they made me feel good with their words they said, their promises they made when they thought they would have something with the beauty from the hood that every man wanted. It sounded good, the picture they painted.

I was clear that touching me was off limits. I wanted to be the one in control of what happened to me, use men for my advantage, and keep them from hurting me anymore. Men seem to like girls who gave it up without a fight but then they treated them like shit afterwards, like they were a hoe, nothing to them but an easy lay.

I didn't want to give it up. I didn't want to be treated like shit afterwards. I wasn't a hoe. I wasn't and will never be an easy lay. I wanted to wait until I was married to have sex. I was trying to be something I wasn't and as bad as I was hurting I was causing more harm to myself than others had. I didn't want to continue to try to be something that I wasn't. I was not a rebel and hurting people was not who I was.

After trying to be a rebel I realized I couldn't be that person. I wasn't evil. I wasn't a heart breaker. I didn't want to get close to anyone just to push them away. I didn't want anyone in my space. So, I convinced myself to go back into my shell. Shy away from the world. Just as quick as I convinced myself to stop I was approached by someone I had been trying to manipulate into seeing me, what I thought was the new me. He spoke my name. He said hello. He was a very handsome young man. I smiled, then I started to flirt. He was shy. Very shy. Didn't say a whole lot. He allowed me to lead the conversation.

I think God saved me that day. Saved me from a life of misery. Misery that I would have ended up bringing to myself. Misery that I would have allowed others to bring into my life. I wasn't a rebel. Well, I may be a rebel in some things in life but not a rebel that would bring pain to myself and others. I ended up falling in love and marrying that young man. My mind was focused on him, loving him, being with him and allowing him to love me just as I was with all my flaws, past hurt. All the pain that remain he eased.

My life was changed with a simple hello. But I truly believe if I didn't have that brief moment trying to be a rebel in life, manipulating people with my charm, he may not have had the courage to say hello. To me that was God intervening in my life to save me. True love saved me. The children we had saved me. That day was the beginning of an amazing future for me that I had no sight to before. I stopped focusing on the pain. I stopped focusing on the past so much and started focusing on my future. My dreams were vivid. God gave me a journey in life that was leading me towards my future, towards my right now.

That simple hello gave me courage.

That simple hello gave me a new life.

That simple hello allowed me to love me.

That simple hello gave me myself back.

I was changed that day. I thank God for that hello. I was given so many blessings after that day that have touched my heart and changed my life forever. I knew exactly what love felt like. I knew what being in love felt like. I knew what loving a child felt like. I knew what having a child to love you back felt like.

I knew love.

Hello love.

So glad to finally meet true love.

Wow! Love felt amazing.

Although me and Mr. Hello didn't last forever it was a time I am grateful for, that I thank God for. My children are my life, my reason, my heart, my blessings from God that saved me, gave me a reason to continue to want to give love, receive love, live in love. They made me want to make all my dreams come true, to be a leader for them, to set examples and teach them the things I wished I had seen and been taught.

I was now living for them to live.

That moment of being a rebel led me to a life worth living for. Led me to a love worth having, worth feeling, worth giving. I don't want to imagine my life if I continued to not care, not love, not give a damn about myself or others. I am sure it would have been a disastrous life, a life not worth claiming.

Thank God for simple hello's that change lives, that start new beginnings. That day my life was saved. My life was changed.

Chapter 20

My Beauty My Curse

My beauty was my curse as I grew up in a world that didn't love me back, that didn't love me for who I was, who God made me to be. Maybe it was God's way of keeping me humble, keeping me from thinking I could have anything in the world because of my looks. It may work like that for some people who God didn't give my purpose, my talents, my gifts. But God did give me my gifts to use for His purpose, to change lives, save lives, inspire others to keep on living, keep on fighting, keep on believing in who God made them to be.

My beauty was my curse because people who didn't understand me hated me because of how I looked. They didn't look like me, they didn't get all the "unwanted" attention like me, they didn't have the confidence to walk, speak, act like I did because they feared what someone would say or do. I too feared what someone would say or do to me. I just didn't care so much at that time. I was used to being free to be me. But moving somewhere new appeared to destroy me and my confidence. It destroyed me being free. I was now like a caged bird wanting to escape, dreaming of escaping, imagining how it felt to be free. But I was lost in a world where I felt like I didn't belong.

My beauty was a curse to me because men felt like they had a right to overpower me and take what they wanted from me. They made me feel like my beauty was a reason that my "no" didn't mean no to them. That my stop fueled them to keep going, keep taking. That my kindness meant I was willing to easily give up a part of me. My beauty was a reason for me to be touched, talk nasty to, rape.

Just because I was beautiful in the eyes of those who saw me as so, I felt like that brought about hate, pain, lies, pretend love, heart ache to my life. All I wanted was to be free. Free to be me in my own skin. I didn't think I was so beautiful. I often felt like I was ugly and flawed. I felt like I was doing something wrong. I even stopped combing my hair cute, wore baggy clothes that weren't cute. But none of that seemed to matter. It sent a different message that I wasn't loved, that I didn't love myself, I didn't care about myself. I became an easier target. I couldn't win in any situation.

My beauty was my curse. All I wanted to do was be myself. Maybe if I had a mother to teach me how to not care what others thought about me, to love me enough to care and set a better example so I could see what it looked like, I would have been stronger, wiser, more confident. Maybe if I would have had a father there to defend me, teach me about boys, teach me how to be a lady and avoid situations. If I had a daddy in my life, maybe that would have made boys/men afraid to do something to me because they would have known my daddy didn't play those types of games about his daughter and he would come for them. Maybe I would have been protected.

I would avoid situations in life where someone would say I was the prettiest. I didn't want others to hate me or feel intimidated. I just wanted to be friendly, be liked by those I liked, be understood. I wanted to be free to be me, dance and let my hair flow free, smile and have fun without someone saying I was stuck up or thought I was better. I was just being me.

My beauty was my curse, but it taught me how to keep my guard up when needed. How to love those that didn't deserve my love less. How to let go of stuff from those who tried to hurt me for their own selfish gains, because of their own insecurities. It taught me how to love harder with those who deserved my love. I learned so much along my journey that made me a stronger, more courageous, and all around better person, mother, and wife.

I was able to find myself and love myself even when others didn't love me. I found myself avoiding bad relationships and embracing the ones that were good for me, for my children. I experienced true love in life and I am living now in a relationship that is surrounded with love, true love. I am able to allow my current and forever husband to love me whole heartedly and give him all of my love in return. True love is an amazing feeling when you are giving it and receiving it.

My beauty may have been my curse, but now my beauty is embraced, enjoyed, admired by my husband, my children, those who appreciate me for me. My beauty is reflected outside as well as inside my heart. That's all that matters to me. My journey was full of pain, but my beginning of forever is full of happiness.

Find hope in your past experiences they can lead you to a better future. A happier future. Your past does not define who you are right now or who you will become tomorrow. Love you and all the beauty you possess inside and outside. Don't allow pain to keep you from being free to be who you are, who God uniquely made you to be. Beauty is in the eye of the beholder and the eye of the one who possess the beauty they have. Be beautiful, you are beautiful. Own it. Walk in it. Be it!

Beauty is not a curse but indeed a gateway to something more in life.

Chapter 21
Let's Take a Moment

Letter to Parents

Parents, LOVE your children in every aspect of the word love. Affection, attention, protection, life lessons, actions, teachings, with words. Children grow inside the womb of their mothers. They depend on their parents to nurture them, care for them, protect them and teach them how to live life. It is your job to raise your children to be better than you were. You may not know all of the answers but learn how to be a better parent for your child, to your child.

If you didn't have the best upbringing in life to learn from your own parents, then surround yourself with other parents who are doing a good job raising their children. Watch parenting shows, movies that depict positive family interaction. A few of my favorite movies are "Cheaper by the Dozen 1 & 2," "Yours Mine & Ours," and even "Big Momma House 2." It shows how chaotic life can be raising children, but also how being there, teaching them, and love conquers parenting. Or what about "Home alone" where the little boy thinks no one cares about him and he ends up finding out just how much his family loves him, and care for him. Everyone who belongs in a family wants to feel love.

Every family is different in the way they raise children, teach life's lessons, love and care for one another. Sometimes it is said that the ways of a family are just "understood." But what about that one person, your child, who does not understand. Are you just going to assume that because your parents didn't say I love you, didn't show affection, didn't give you the teachings that you thought you needed but instead learned the hard way through living life, that your child understands because that's how life is and was for you?

DON'T ASSUME!

Every child is different and needs something different. Break those generational curses that hinder you from being better. A better mother to your children. A better father to your children. Do those things you desired to have done as a child. Give the hugs you never received. Give the pep talks you never received. Give the tough love to protect you child that you never received. Be a better parent for your child.

There is no perfect parenting way. There is no one book that can teach you everything you should know about parenting or prepare you for what will, may, or could happen. You just have to try to be a good parent for your children. Start with loving them.

Love them with your words.

Love them with understanding.

Love them with affection.

Love them with listening.

Love them with conversations.

Love them by being there and assuring them that they know that you are there no matter what. Love them with laughter. Everything don't always have to be so serious. Love them with fun times even if you don't spend a dime to have the fun. Love them with memories that you make together.

Find what works best for you and your family and be there, show up, talk, give hugs, be kind and fill your heart with love in everything that you say and do. Be a better parent for your child.

Very, very, very, very important parents.

Protect your child from predators. Predators don't wear a sign they say they are one. Little girls shouldn't be left alone with men who are not their father, or any man that you do not trust with your life. Use your instincts. If they are to be left alone with a man, even little boys being left alone, pay attention to them and their behavior. Pay attention to changes. Listen and ask questions. Be smart in your decisions and don't be selfish in your reasoning for leaving your child with just anyone. That club will be open another night. There will be more concerts to attend. Your job is just a job. But your child needs you to see what they can't see. Your child needs you to protect them from the men and women who prey on children. Your child needs you to put them first and protect them with every being in your body.

Your child is yours for life and your responsibility to protect.

Be there for your children.

Love your children.

Talk to your children.

Listen to your children.

Don't be quick to judge or react.

Understand your child's needs.

Understand your child is unique.

Look for drastic change in their attitude, walk, body, behavior.

Ask questions.

Give hugs.

Say I love you!

Parents, your children need you more than anyone else they will ever need in life. You are their beginning. You set the foundation that will guide the rest of their life. Build that foundation. Protect your child. Love your child and be there for YOUR child. They need you, trust me, they do!

Chapter 22
His Plan His Purpose My life

I was abused as a child. I was mistreated as a child. I was abandoned as a child. I was hurt as a child. I was broken as a child. I was lost as a child. But my childhood does not define my right now. My teenage years does not define my right now. My young adulthood does not define my right now. My yesterday does not define my right now.

God.

I remember crying wondering why God allowed things to happen to me. Bad things. I went through fazes of denial, depression, sadness and often was anti-social shutting out everyone around me. Then I think about how God brought me through it all and the woman I am today. Beautiful Curse. That's what I felt like a beautiful girl who was cursed with something that should be a gift, but so many bad things happened to me because of it. A lot of times I didn't even think I was pretty. When people would stare, I felt insecure that they were staring at my truth. I feared they would see and acknowledge my ugly truths and see the lack of beauty that I saw.

But God didn't make me ugly. God didn't make you ugly. His children are all unique and beautiful. His children are made in his perfect image!

I almost died when I was a little girl. I was seven years old and diagnosed with Bacterial Meningitis. When I kept asking my mom what was wrong with me, why I felt so sick, she told me I had a little bug inside my back that was so small that nobody could see it and the doctor had to get it out. I hated bugs. Still do today. Maybe that's why. Didn't think about the reason for my fear of bugs until this very moment. A bug almost claimed my life.

But those words got me up out of bed so that my mom could take me to the doctor. I remember being so sick like it was yesterday. I remember getting to the hospital and the doctor asking me what my favorite food was. I wasn't eating anything. I was too weak. I didn't have an appetite. I told him it was spaghetti. Then he asked me if he brought a pot of spaghetti into the room would I eat it. I remember telling him no. Next thing I know there were seven doctors and nurses holding my body down so they could stick this big long ass needle in my back. I screamed so loud. My mom said her heart broke because she couldn't do anything to save me. I remember it like it was yesterday.

I was so mad at those doctors. I was so mad at those nurses. I was so mad at my mom. I was mad. I didn't understand that they were trying to help me. I didn't understand that I had to go through that pain in order for me to heal, to become better, to be better.

Think about the pain in your life. It will make you better.

I don't remember a lot about what happened at the hospital. I remember waking up and I was in a hospital bed in a room and my entire body hurt. It hurt when I moved. I couldn't walk. I could barely move from side to side. I stayed in the hospital for a couple weeks. The doctors told my mom that I could have died. I was not supposed to make it.

But God!

God had a purpose for me being here. God needed me to go through all the pain I endured at age seven and after that. God needed me to hurt. God needed me to experience what so many young girls have and still are experiencing. He knew I was strong enough to handle it even if I didn't think I was strong at all.

God needed me to share my testimony to save someone's daughter from experiencing any of what I experienced. To save someone's mother or father from lacking the ability to protect their daughter.

God needed me to save someone's life.

DON'T YOU DARE GIVE UP!

God is not done with you yet!

God has a purpose for you too!

You are not alone.

God loves you and so do I!

God saved my life over and over. He kept me safe even when I didn't feel like he was keeping me safe. God gave me tears to cry to make me stronger. He never took away my love but instead he kept my heart full.

I almost died.

I could have died.

But my purpose was not fulfilled. He didn't let me go. He saved me. He loved me. I was enough for him to save. I didn't realize it back then what He was doing but I am grateful that even when I didn't know, God knew.

So, I share this testimony today in hopes of helping someone get through and overcome rape, molestation, abuse. I share my stories and hope that some mother will read and save her daughter from harm, or simply listen and not jump to conclusion when she tries or needs to tell you she was raped. And if she does, that you will hold her in your arms tight. Tighter. Her tears need to flow. Her pain needs to start healing and a mother's love has a healing power that is out of this world, so amazingly super powerful.

No matter what you have been through, God has a way to help overcome IT and use your testimony for His glory and for your success.

My God.

God knows my strengths and He wouldn't put anything on me that I couldn't bear. Same goes for you, God knows your strengths. My past is my past, and my right now is who I am. No weapon formed against me shall prosper. Love yourself enough to know that you do matter, and you are enough.

God has a plan for your life. Your struggles are not in vain. Your heart ache is not in vain. Your pain was not, is not in vain. Pray to God your desires. Pray to God for understanding. Pray to God for clear direction to your purpose in life. Walk not in fear but in faith that God has you and will lead you towards your chosen path.

I didn't understand His purpose then, but I surely understand now. God equipped me with the armor I needed to survive my journey. He gave me the tools I needed, the gifts I needed, the wisdom I needed, to guide me on my journey of life that leads to purpose, God's purpose. Don't allow life to defeat you when God's glory for your life is so much greater.

God has a plan for you. God has a purpose for you. God has a journey for you to take in life that comes together to make you stronger, make you better, and equip you with the armor that will guide your better future.

Trust in Him.

Lean on Him

Believe in Him.

God is Love and Love is God.

His Plan. His Purpose. My Life.

Your Life!

Chapter 23
Letter To you, Young Girls

This is my heartfelt letter to all the Young Girls in the world. If I could have written a letter to my younger self I would have written the letter, sealed it up and placed it in so many places for me to find to remind me of my gifts, my qualities, and to tell me what I should or shouldn't do in life. I would warn me of bad situations, tell me what type of men to avoid and how to live a happier, successful life. But since I can't write my younger self a letter, here is my letter to all of you instead.

Dear Young Girl, one day some terrible things may happen to you, but I want to help you try and avoid some of those bad things and if you can't, I want to help you cope the best way possible. Everything that will happen to you in life will guide you towards a better tomorrow, a better you, and a better life in your future.

First thing first, always love yourself just as you are and know that God made you perfect. God don't make any mistakes, so you my dear are no mistake, instead you are one of His greatest blessings. Always remember that you are special, and you are important in this world. Nothing that could ever happen to you or be said to you would change that fact. Greedy people will try to take from you, will try to break you, will try to make you feel like you are not worthy enough to exist, to love, to feel any type of emotion or be allowed to be amazing. YOU ARE AMAZING!

You may not see all of your God given talents yet, but trust me when I say you have been blessed with some amazing gifts from God. Even when you think He is not there, trust and know that HE is watching over you, He is protecting you from His children who have lost their way, who have chosen to be evil and do evil to you. You are valuable to God. You are valuable to yourself, to your future self, to your future purpose. You are highly valuable!

Remember that NO MEANS NO ALWAYS! There is never an exception to when it doesn't mean no. Try not to ever put yourself in a situation where someone may try to take advantage of you. If someone wants you to do something that makes you feel uncomfortable, don't hesitate to "not go," don't hesitate to remove yourself from that situation. Listen to your gut. Be smart and try to get out of a situation unharmed. NO ALWAYS MEAN NO. No exceptions.

When you are at parties watch what you are drinking, you don't want anyone spiking your drink attempting to take advantage of you. Have a buddy system with friends, keep a reliable someone's number on speed dial in case of an emergency. Don't leave a club with a man if you don't plan on having sex with him. Just because he paid for you a drink or two or three doesn't mean you have to sleep with him. Watch your surroundings and where you go. If you feel uneasy, go the opposite way and find a place where you feel safe.

Try to always prevent bad situations. But if you find yourself in a bad situation, try your best to get out of it and remember to protect yourself first. Sometimes when we are faced with bad situations we wish we could magically disappear from them, but when it is happening think survival. When you make it out of a bad situation, use it as a learning lesson to protect yourself in the future. Use it as a teaching lesson to save someone else from the same evil situation.

Listen to your mother when they say no. They often are speaking from experience and know more than what they may say to you out loud. No doesn't mean they are keeping you from having fun, it may be keeping you out of harm's way.

Sleep overs are not always fun. Point. Blank. Period. Parents can't protect you from the perverts that lurk at your friend's homes. Perverts look like law abiding citizens out in public. Evil wears a mask of kindness and friendliness around others.

Speak up louder when you are not being heard. If your parents are not hearing you speak louder to let them know you are hurting or needing to be heard. Speak up louder about the harm you face, the bad things that have happened to you. Just say the words out loud. Say them loud and clear. If not to your parents, then to some trusted person who can and will protect you.

Ask questions when you don't know. Don't be afraid to ask. Even if you feel embarrassed or unsure of the response. You will never know what you may receive in a response if you don't ask. Sometimes parents may not know what to say or tell you until you ask.

Take care of your personal hygiene. Make sure you are clean, take baths daily. Make sure your private areas are always clean, shave under your arms and down below, keep your private areas well groomed. Make sure your hair is clean, wash it, condition it, and combed your hair. Your finger nails and hands should always be clean. Make sure you smell good, even if all you have is soap and water. Love yourself enough to take care of your personal hygiene. Be clean.

Make yourself look and feel beautiful and don't allow others to make you feel any less so that they can feel as if they are better than you or prettier than you. Your beauty is your blessing. Your beauty is yours and you don't have to apologize for the gifts and blessings that God has given you!

When life seems hard, find something greater inside you to hold on to. Get lost in music, writing, reading, or whatever it is that can occupy your mind until you can get back to believing in you enough to know that your pain is fuel for your future. Your right now is temporary and will define your tomorrow, will make you stronger, will become a part of your purpose in life, will build you up to be wiser, smarter, and become a better you!

You are enough!

You are valuable! You are Gods child, a unique design that He created perfectly in His image. Protect yourself. Love yourself. Always be good to yourself. You deserve the best of you! You deserve to overcome and live a life of greatness, to dream an amazing dream and build a future that you can be proud of and one day look back and know that your past never defined your future. Your right now won't last long, your tomorrow is waiting on you, and your future YOU is waiting for you to overcome and keep living life to get to your best you yet!

Life doesn't stop when bricks and stones are thrown at you, or mountains come crumbling down, but the way you stand tall in your truth of who you are and Whose you are, and keep on giving the best you, keep on loving yourself, keep on praying for your better tomorrow, and walk in God's purpose for your life will impact your journey for the greatness God has planned for you. Your greatest blessings in life are coming, your better days are coming, your breakthrough is coming, healing and deliverance is coming! Be strong and keep fighting for you, keep fighting for your future. You are enough! You are worthy! You are a blessing from God. You are blessed with a brighter future. Don't you dare give up! Don't you dare!

P.S.

You will love who you become! You are not a Beautiful Curse!